So I See

Jesse McGunnigle

PublishAmerica
Baltimore

First printing

PublishAmerica has allowed this work to remain exactly as the author intended, verbatim, without editorial input.

Hardcover 978-1-4489-1231-5
Softcover 1-60836-756-8
PUBLISHED BY PUBLISHAMERICA, LLLP
www.publishamerica.com
Baltimore

Printed in the United States of America

For Tobias.

Thank you for helping me be me. And for the extra pair of eyes when I need them.

1

"Do you know why the pudding's rat race is never on ice?" the man in gray asked, as though the answer would simply astound me.

The turbulence of the day had been more than enough to fill my head with dispersions of all sorts, yet this gentleman's small talk felt it necessary to play an integral part in solidifying my madness. I could not begin to understand how he failed to see that I was in no mood or condition to reciprocate, nor delight, in such disposable conversation.

"Do I know why the pudd—"

"No you don't, because neither do I!" This absolutely thrilled him, though I doubt he rightfully knew why.

I had never imagined that casual chitchat could evoke murderous caprice in my head, but there I was, wishing this man to either swallow his every desire to speak, or to die at my own hands. I imagined he felt me to be most delinquent in my return effort, but I had done nothing to encourage him to begin with. And while I willingly admit my hand in stimulating mindless banter from time to time, there are moments of notable contrast when the levels of patience and courtesy are tested, tried, and hung.

So when was it that I so easily wanted to kill a man for merely commenting that the night had been a hot one? An admirable one? One which we would soon yearn for in the aftermath of winter's opening act? Why, of course, the day that I could no longer trust my eyes. A day whose birth began with the unrelenting cries of a sunshine whose refusal to be denied triumphed over the blinds and curtains of the city, and into the hearts of the sleeping and freshly awaken.

Bright. The first word that came to mind that morning as I coaxed my eyes into action, my fluffy head on a heavy pillow, or did I have that wrong? I had just woken up. I winced and scoffed at the idea that my shades were, in fact, room darkening as they had promised—a rather redundant claim by my estimation—while watching the infinite number of dust pellets float with glee through the thin beam of white light that snuck into my room, much like children in a sprinkler on a hot summer day.

I wrestled with my blankets, fighting routine, and asked for another fate, another destiny, another anything you please. My appeal was denied and I mournfully fell in step, rising to eat, shower, and trudge through another five hour work day which I did(yawn) before wrapping it all up with a jog in the park.

What say you, legs?

I had to ask, you see, for the solicitation of my legs to adhere to my wishes, that of a mere jog in the park, commences often times with respectful yet uninterested obligation, while others with the exuberance of a freshly lit bottle rocket. Still, either way, we go on. A cog in a well planned and structured routine, my evening jaunts had for many years served to exonerate the crimes of the day committed inexcusably against me—the first always being the mocking, unadulterated cry of a device whose sole purpose being to dip ever so disconcertedly into man's soul and demand that he cast off his dealings with the abstract colony in the arcane slumber which he temporarily resides; fused to the end of that rope noodling down the well, the severed head of the fervid ecstasies in which such surreal reality is achieved so acceptingly and without stiff regard for self-consciousness. I speak, of course, of the devil's jack-in-the-box, the rooster's lightning rod, the webbed hand cast upon a pale shoulder: the alarm clock. Could there possibly breathe a more profane means to unwrapping a freshly baked day? The device's very existence is a crime, and such a crime does not hesitate in making acquaintances with other unruly acts: the cold that seizes one upon stepping out of the shower, bread that stales before its expiration date, a new pen whose ink will not flow, or being forced to succumb to tantalizing minuets of traffic whose rude backside greets your weary eyes at each bookend of the work day (whose unspeakable crimes should more than account for any which one should have to undergo in order to stake instrumental claim amongst the countless herd that cultivate the capitalist landscape and breathe life into the economic bull—ruler of the workforce minions, taking casualties and brides at whim).

Now while I do wake to the fissure of an alarm clock, I do not think it fair to claim to be amid these malleable sheep, as my money comes from rewards of countless brushstrokes, the abstract memories which stain a virgin canvas. I do not have to fight traffic with them, and I do not rot in a walled square space designated for the eradication of one's soul. I paint, and if so inclined you could call me a painter, or an artist if you prefer. Either way, people will hear this, generalize, and assume that I either paint houses or that I am unemployed and writing a book which will never be published.

Still, my dealings with these mislead and overly motivated soldiers of consumption, I feel, entitles me to wear the mask of weariness, of sacrifice, and dine with the same utensils necessary to properly inhale the fodder which feeds the mite of lamentation. And as I declare this, I am reminded that our paths were the same for a long time, our sugary cravings, our ends the same burnt match! I, too, fed the mite. And not very long ago. I wish I could blame this on poor prescription glasses, but seeing as I own not a single pair, this claim would hold nothing. I wish blindness were the culprit, for who then could argue confidently that I should have seen the errors I propagated! Unfortunately my own decadence, living under asylum at this time, bears sole responsibility for living such a life…

September came in true New England fashion that year: packing a light sweater. A weather forecaster with moderate consistency could find themselves a messiah in these parts, but I have never known such folk to exist. I vaguely recall someone wishing me a happy "September Day" in a tone suggesting they were altogether proud of their cleverness. I am certain I offered at the very least a smile, or a 'right back atcha' to vindicate their effort; yes, it's true, I am kind to the awkward and the walking, talking, dead who roam unaware of their condition. Poor souls.

So as habit would demand, I set out for my daily run at the same time the downtown restaurants begin setting up their tables, along the vast river that helped shape the precious little city I called home. The air that wafted over and into the paved path which ran parallel to the water promised smiles inside and out to those sprinkled by it. I have always enjoyed the aroma it delivered and could now feel its freshness in my eyes, my sight seeming endless. Conditions were optimal for flying, or in my case running, and the cotton candy skies echoed the sun's sweet taste.

My mouth was emptied and then filled with determination, each pursed breath measuring the impending end of the jagged bank, nearly a mile and a half in length. The park which ran alongside was fitted with joggers, rollerbladers, walkers, truck vendors, picnickers, and other assorted characters, all whose animations were a stark contrast to the finely manicured paths accentuated with wood and wrought iron benches, water bubblers, and inconspicuous trash barrels housed in enclosures surely the envy of the scarce homeless to be found.

Oh how their minds must have ached at the sights of the immeasurable displays of waste and lavish uselessness that surrounded them!

Too selfish to care at the time, I often found myself offended or put off by the eyes of those whose tales of woe now humbly remind me how fragile and fleeting life's opportunities can be. There were likely one or two of these unfortunate souls within eyeshot as I made my way amongst the other health conscious peoples, but the many swaying trees which covered the park overshadowed their forced indifference, their clipped wings ensuring their place within obscurity.

Perched beneath a small section of these trees sat a coy collection of chess tables and benches to match. Yes, you could actually play chess on the benches, if you pleased. The weather was always frightful on the rarest of days when these tables were actually empty. I personally lacked the patience or appreciation for the game of chess, which always seemed to attract a rather serene crowd from one day to the next. I did, however, envy the peace of mind I perceived its chessy participants to have, and hoped that for me, chess was not the answer to slaying the elusive dragon head of tranquility. And that I could continue to use the word chessy without a mind from anyone.

Well, there they were, gathered there as scheduled, smiles from onlookers and the furrowed brows of those deep in thought as to what to do. Chess was all about what to do. When it's your turn, or not, what to do, oh what to do. It had crossed my mind on several occasions to drop in and play a game or two sometime, although I was certain I would meet my demise if I had to challenge any of the seasoned veterans frequenting these particular tables. A child of say, six, might have been a better match for someone of my skill level. And while I passed them on that fateful day, their place in the park comforted me, as often things that were consistent did.

Little did I know that before long I would be on the ground, surrounded by their musk, and helplessly praying for their help.

I concede that the malodorous breaths exhaled buy the oblivious masses have indeed long been a peevish occurrence, or transpiration, in my day to day musings. Surely gum and breath mints—not to mention the toothbrush—could not be in such short supply as these mouths would have me believe. Hygiene, that is all I am saying. Well, crafty as I can be at times, I have managed to adapt a series of expressions and movements to combat the projection of these foul exhalations, although waking from an unplanned, unconscious state on your back does not allow for such strategic tactics. I noted this quite quickly as I came to and searched for my whereabouts, the rigid grass tickling the exposed lower portion of my back, as well as my wrists and hands.

A husky voice rattled my focus and its vapors sought to purloin my relief at wakening.

"C'mon fella, wasted light shines upon you, come back and let it in," the elder man spoke softly or loudly whispered, I couldn't be sure which he was going for. Nor could I be sure which tea bag he had read that from, and I silently noted that it best suited an inspirational leaflet aimed at someone freshly removed from a tragedy, overcoming an addiction—or even for someone just dug out of a long winter's nap. Regardless, I was in no mood for spiritual metaphors or uplifting sermons to help rekindle my senses.

The gruff tones, however, ceased to sense this preference of mine.

"Grasp the songs you heard with your eyes, for those are true melodies, their pitch impeccable." I actually laughed out loud, a chortled cough, and sat up to find a laundry sack of a man kneeling over me, smiling as though he had just resuscitated me from a water related mishap. I secretly hoped our lips hadn't touched, and after searching my own with my tongue for a lingering kiwi skinned leftover, assumed I was safe. The overall composition of brown haired fruit both offended me and scattered ants up the arch of my back.

Chilled sweat sank down my face as I let the volume of the world adjust to my ears, the cars racing to their destinations, only to start all over again, the commoners performing their walking, talking, and running rituals, and the birds laughing at our expense, high overhead.

It was apparent, when my thoughts caught up with my senses, that I had ended up on my backside thanks to a series of hallucinations I experienced not long before. The faces which surrounded me, logging my confused expressions, seemed to be caring ones, soft and firm as a good night tuck can be.

The tables had been abandoned, battles delayed until orders delivered to return to war. I wondered if any of them had thought to cheat while the stranger on the ground selfishly utilizing their precious time regained his bearings. The carved participants in these battles, sitting atop the checkered tables, showed Zen-like patience, unaffected by the trivial doings of people, their demeanors void of a pulse.

A tattered man (clutching a dark wooden cane which seemed more for effect than to sturdy, as it was waved around with the ease of a baton) whose clothes hung as if sleeping, nudged his way to the front of the modest crowd of ten or twelve and kindly asked if I cared for a sampling of his porridge. Yes, the man used just that word!

"Do I wa—" I hesitatingly began to ask, unsure of the helpfulness a hot pile of porridge—which seemed to smell an awful lot like chili—could offer, but was quickly cut off by the sincerity and calm of a voice only a woman could tender.

"No, Charlie, he doesn't want—" The elder, soft skinned woman caught herself before finishing the absurd thought, opting to kneel beside me to offer a bottle of water fetched from an ice filled cooler nearby. "Don't listen to him. An absolute darling, but helpful as two sets of lips." I pondered the thought and decided two sets of lips could have many advantages, yet I understood her no less. A small smile curled its way to the front of my face as I looked up at the pretty gray-green eyes, plucked from the bed of an emerald sea, concerned with my plight.

"Thank you so much," I thanked her with my voice and eyes and sipped the water which struck my throat with a thousand spades.

"Honey, do you remember what happened?" Her voice. I could listen to it all day! "You were begging us to help make it stop. Make what stop, dear?" she asked, rubbing my leg gently, and I wondered what she had looked like thirty years ago. Her concerned stare, encased by dark, thinned hair that fell like angels, told me not to be afraid, to confess what had come so violently over me, but my embarrassment and disbelief had other ideas, and a much safer, more acceptable story left my mouth.

"There was this terrible, crippling, high pitched noise in

my ears." I sighed with a weighted shrug, and sipped the water to help my explanation appear more believable. "I can't even begin to tell you how bad it was, I just wanted it to stop. Sorry, if I frightened or bothered anyone. First time that's happened." This much was true, the details mattered not. I most likely would never speak to these people again, although I knew my daily run would surely have to include the occasional wave and smile to this group, or else forever be labeled rude and thoughtless.

I was received with nods and assurances that I was no trouble, that they were glad to come to my aid, and if need be they would be there again if such luck should befall me. I was told not to worry, that I was most likely dehydrated, and before long the episode would be forgotten, the eyes of charity at hand but a fleeting memory logged in a miscellaneous file someplace poorly lit.

Yet another cane-bearing elder chimed in his tea leaf wisdom: "Son, is it possible the noise you hear is the sound of the end of your limits, and to push yourself beyond them is a sacred danger to you? Is chasing that jumping-bean dollar with your every desires flicker worth the price?"

I hadn't expected this out of his dried, wrinkly mouth, which seemed to be filled with rocks, or a swollen cough drop, and I wasn't sure how to respond. This old man did not know me from the drool on his chin, yet he was so easily lumped me with the crowd that kept this city sleeping with one eye on the door and one hand on the snooze button. I figured it was the watch I wore that drove him to such a conclusion; however, I doubted he would know the difference between it and a sundial. The crisp, bright blue denim jacket he wore looked stiff as if newly dry cleaned, contrary to its natural design, while the matching jeans appeared equally rigid and discomforting. I could hardly take the outfit seriously, so how was I expected to take its owner any more so? I decided there was no point in answering this line of questioning with substance. I looked to his head, half-expecting a matching hat, but came up empty.

"I suppose anything is possible," I answered with a surprised look, pushing myself to my feet. What if he was right? I labored hard at times, yet no more than anyone else around, perhaps even less. Silly little man, what did he know?

"Hard to keep the gas in the Rolls if I let up though!" I joked, my jest lost on the huddled assembly, while saddened expressions tried themselves out on me. I decided to make my exit before a group hug ensued.

I finished the second half of the clear bottle with a single, swift dose and held it up to thank its delivery person. The kind old woman, clad in a soft blue velvet-skinned running suit with a little embroidered something-or-other on the left hip, returned my thanks with a mouthed "you're welcome" and the cutest, bashful smile which seemed to tell me that it wasn't too late—or early—in life to make new friends or try new things. My weakened condition had left my thinking skewed, so I dismissed the mischief brewing before being bitten by its vampire charm.

On my feet, I surveyed the immediate surroundings. I checked to see if those beyond the chess club confines were interested in the dramatic happenings. Luckily enough, the few that passed were too involved in their own activities to waste any energy upon a bechanced runner and his dusty collection of rescuers.

I squinted hard, trying to rid the sting of sweat piercing my eyes. The pain reminded me that I was not off the hook for whatever I had done to deserve this fate, an unlucky bingo card gone up in flames to the delight of the winner whose prize helps to fill the ceramic kitten atop the refrigerator undoubtedly caked with a layer of grease and grime.

I announced my plans to depart for home, and panned the ground for any personal affects I might have left behind, prompting a return visit I hoped to avoid. To my left, a well wisher voiced his concern, advising that I charter a taxi for the ride home. He pushed his way over to me, intrusively close in order to show his face so that I might read the concern scrawled across it. I managed to circumvent the possibility of his foul breath after smelling the moth balls he surely had been hiding in his pockets. I imagined his voice to taste none better and bent over, putting my hands down on my knees, my head following suit. I looked up to see his overly tanned, scruff face, which surely at one time had served him well with the women of his day, although now it made him look weathered, lazy, and unkempt.

"I think I'll be alright. The fresh air will do me good." It is amazing what a sampling of fresh air can do. Sick to your stomach? Get some fresh air. A long stressful day at the office? Go on and get some fresh air. Surrounded by geriatric folk whose prolonged presence is making you more and more uncomfortable? Surely the solution is a bout of fresh air!

The idea of the fresh, free, and abundant air seemed amenable to everyone in attendance, so I thanked them one final time and a chorus of goodbyes, good lucks, and good tidings bounced off my shoulder and back as I walked away. I examined my hands and noted they were mine.

2

The same night of the very day my feet appeared to be giving birth to more feet, I found myself on the backend of two bottles of pinot noir, sharing a sofa with a fetching brunette I had met only hours before. The same laugh which had earlier encouraged my incontinence I now found to be a justifiable excuse for homicide, although my penchant for exaggeration may be speaking here.

You must understand that I often manage to involve myself in situations whose blueprints I scripted from the ground up, yet whose destruction can never seem to come swiftly enough to my satisfaction. The ever far-reaching quest for curious thrill, instant gratification, and ultimate happiness is in itself a hindrance whose nectar I use to guide my progress through the world. So? How does that differ from anyone else? Well, I suppose it doesn't, but regardless of the danger this compass should lead me, there is a certain transcendence I allow it over reason (for my well being) and more often than not I wish I had allowed myself more patience with the desires I covet, or at the least some sensibility in my decision making. What wins out more often than not is the reminder that in so many instances, my desires are fulfilled and noted, serving their purpose—of perseverance, infiltration, and occupation—but ultimately I am no better, or happier, or wiser.

Time and time again, boredom has been the driving force, persistently managing to elude reason and convince my conscious that regardless of all possible consequences, the risks taken and the pleasures (if even for a passing moment) outweigh the pains which could likely result from the pursuit of the implied prizes (which, in retrospect lack the ephemeral bliss their fruition promised).

There have also been times, although of rare breed, where defensive logic has won out over my want, freeing me from sure regret, and in that moment the relief I feel in avoiding inevitable disaster rinses the whole thought process. I travel from start to finish, and like a strong breeze that knocks the hat from your head, I experience the highs and lows of the idea, relieved and pleased to know I possess the whereabouts to overcome that which I romanticized with sound, convenient reasoning.

Other times, as in this night, I merely play along. I have no plan, no ultimate desire, no scheme, no wish other than new experience—or the refraction of boredom—and I am simply dealt into strange situations. I do not question my intentions, or those of my counterparts, although perhaps I should, and I let chance and the pinwheel of life determine the outcome. I suppose every day we all end up in situations, some more eventful than others, by I feel as though I tend to end up in those of the most precarious nature more often than the standard barnyard raccoon.

She had been the clerk at the liquor store I visited on the way back to my house, and her inviting curves were enough to make any man forget that he might just be losing touch with the harsh realities of the world around him and the cavalier means by which he plays checkers with it. Or maybe just me.

"So what had you all shaken up earlier?" she asked, curled up beside me on her thick black sofa whose cushions threatened to swallow me whole, squeezing my hand just enough to exhibit her concern. "I was afraid to ask, but you looked like you had seen a ghost when you first walked in. I figured you were having withdrawals, or fleeing the scene, or something. Then you went and made a mess!"

It seemed safe enough to tell her the truth, considering there was little chance of her laughing as a result. I tried to keep the tone serious while I was her guest, anything to avoid the pain her cackles sliced into my head. I would not mention details of the clothing donned by my new friends at the river, or the fact that I enjoy maple syrup on my pizza—whatever means necessary to keep me clear of oncoming laughs from my tightly dressed companion. Her name was Hannah, and still would be today if she had not met me.

I told her that I had gone for my daily run, and that it was business as usual, until "I felt the early stages of the hunger dizzies."

"The hunger dizzies?" Her laugh stabbed the back of my neck, holes dug out from the inside, behind my ears. I revealed that if I did not eat enough, I grew quite dizzy, a concept I thought self-explanatory by its name. By now I had already determined this woman not to be a budding scientist or philosopher, and the befuddlement at ideas like this further cemented this perception. Her shortcomings, however, were heavily outweighed by the taut, black stretch pants she wore, much to my acceptance. Plus, her name was a palindrome, and how much fun was *that*?

As I continued, I saw one of two scenarios playing themselves out. The first, tasting very much the way a cinnamon roll and a glass of milk does on an empty stomach, would have had myself and Hannah trying to procure fire with our bodies after she learned of the day I had and her nurturing instincts took hold. The second would find me driving home unsatisfied, wishing I had concocted a similar tale to the one I told the elders earlier that day involving random noise in my ear. Either way, I was not overly concerned with the outcome. I felt well, relaxed, and relieved, thanks to the wine, and very little—with the exception of a repeat of earlier events—could do much to change that.

Now I cannot admit to being infinitely intrigued by this

woman, although she did offer up some interesting ideas on love, explaining that she did not believe in marriage, because she could not trust her own heart.

"It has a mind of it's own, I have no control of it, no matter what I tell it I want. It does as it pleases. It's really frustrating!"

"So do you believe you will ever trust it?"

"Do you really trust yours? I bet it's a lying, cheating, throbbing mass like mine." She looked at me, ready to denounce any claim I might lay to my heart's truthfulness. "I'm not saying you can't love, or don't love, but even when you do, is it really your mind that makes your decisions? Or is it your heart?"

I sat up, and shook my head. "You're speaking as if the heart were a separate, thinking organ, and that it transfers its feelings to a part of the brain which has no control over decision making—making it a mere wholesale distributor. I hate to disagree, but the heart you speak of is actually part of your brain, and not as you say a separate perceptive entity such as your tongue or eyes or ears which relay information thus forth."

"Well wherever it is, it doesn't listen very well, so maybe I should get it a hearing aid or something have it implanted into my head with a wire that goes down into my heart. You think they could rig up something like that?"

I looked for the hidden cameras capturing the joke at its climax but found none lurking behind suspect plants or books. I remarked that the hamster wheel in her head was going strong after a couple of bottles of wine, and again her laugh punished me for forgetting its existence. Laughs have been responsible for the downfall of several of my relationships. This isn't to say that a laugh by itself is the one thing that makes or breaks these potential unions, for my fuse is susceptible to tripping by means of other sources; poor kissing, sleeping compatibility, dining etiquette, and a woman's walk all have an equal share in potentially belaying the launching of my romances.

To understand how a woman's walk can be of such importance, one must know that my senses are heightened ones to begin with. The hum and tick of an old toaster are enough for me to envision the same toaster being cast off my second floor balcony in an effort to stop the sounds that refuse to repent while toasting my bread. Some might suggest that merely unplugging the toaster or relocating to another room while toasting would prove a more reasonable solution, yet I argue that those ideas to not take into account the fact that the demise of the toaster would not only solve the problem infinitely, but surely be entertaining as well. Furthermore, tossing the said toaster off my balcony could also gauge the sturdiness and reliability of the toaster, a test I am sure is not administered among their manufacturers.

And as I continue with this idea, I feel that a consulting fee would be more than appropriate should I be asked to conduct such tests with other household items exhibiting the same psychotic tendencies, such as the blender, the refrigerator, coffee maker, and of course the aforementioned alarm clock. I would gladly spend the waking hours of the remainder of my days hurling alarm clocks out windows, down stairs, under moving cars, etc, etc, should such test be deemed necessary, or even if not for that matter.

Moving away from this gabble, and returning to walks, I feel posture to be of the utmost importance, its suggestive power resonates in my mind and either promotes or dissuades certain sexual bubblings. A slouch hints at possible laziness or lack of self-confidence, while an erect walk that flows like rain can suggest confidence that ultimately translates to the bedroom. Foot position can also be troublesome, whereas I can find a pigeon-toed or duck-toed walk absolutely maddening, not because it implies anything of any sort, but rather because such an escape from what my eyes perceive to be normal sets off a feeling of unsteadiness and distaste, one from which I cannot escape.

Do not be mislead to feel that I believe in perfection, or that my attraction to others lies solely in such unrealistic and unfair expectations. This is not the case, and in time I will do my best to explain. I feel to this brief point I may come across a bit superficial, and to an extent I will allow that to be stipulated, for in everyone there are places where the levels of aesthetic pleasantry mold opinion, but please understand that these outward preferences on appearance put forth are not from the heart, but rather direct evaluations of my senses, two altogether different nations with different agendas and complex economies.

My eyes are a device of sight, my mouth of taste. My nose is a device of smell, my ears of hearing. Each with it's own vocation, they do their best to inform my brain what they perceive, and in each person this perception may, and usually is, different to some degree. For the most part the degrees that separate these evaluations in each of us are minimal, and of little consequence, yet as with everything there are exceptions and this is where opinion rears its ugly head and refuses to yield to the crowd that damns its different and seemingly unfound ideas.

Upon walking into the liquor store earlier that day, I was struck by Hannah, her black, endless hair framing eyes which hung low with dark weighted circles that suggested a series of sleepless nights. I found them most arousing. If we were to affix ourselves to the idea that I am only attracted to displays of perfection, that my overly-critical and judgmental ways surely could not find this tired woman attractive, then I would have walked straight to the red wines in the middle aisle instead of knocking over a warm six-pack of spiked lemonade while trying to catch a glimpse of her sad face.

You see, the trivial things in which I place great importance, to me are, in fact, of great importance. To *me,* that is, and I have always failed to see why I must try to compromise these beliefs just to satisfy others whose opinions and realities do not mirror my own. It was not until losing faith in the truth of these realities did I realize this change was necessary for my overall well-being and happiness in the long run, but while I stood over the broken glass and sticky liquid I had freed from bottled confinement, such revelations were far away.

She came walking over, the looks of disgust and inconvenience fighting for the stage on her slightly weathered facade. The paleness of the fleshy paint I wore showed my regret and I apologized, palms together as if in prayer, and asked for a mop. Waving off this idea she turned to her left, revealing a scar on her neck which stung my own upon its sight. She yelled across the room to an imaginary person somewhere in the back, then informed me the stock boy would take care of it as soon as he was done servicing himself—with the aid of a magazine—in the restroom. The vulgarity of her joke was lost on me, as injecting the alcohol into my arm would not have been a quick enough means to intoxication, a state I was in dire need of.

I smirked and apologized again, adding that I was merely looking for a decent bottle of pinot to have with dinner. Inwardly, I remarked it *was* dinner. She surprised me with her knowledge on the matter, although I don't know why, being I was in a liquor store, and suggested a bottle which I gladly had her bag and ring up. She then playfully suggested I join her later to taste a similar serum that she held in her private collection, and I willingly agreed.

Sitting beside her on the sofa, the television's blue glow illuminated the long scar on her neck I believed to be at the hand of a knife, yet imagined to be from the swift graze of a cutlass in a duel. I dared not ask of its source, and wondered if she could sense my thoughts. Instead, I revealed the source of the look of horror I wore when we first met.

A steady, elevated heartbeat, along with the adept work of my legs and controlled breathing, makes for my afternoon jaunt by the water. Always equipped with a trendy and miniscule wireless music delivery device, I envision myself breathing within an external dimension, void of the constrictions and the hypocrisy of the reality in which I choose to spend the other twenty two hours. This day was no different.

Locked in stride and my carriage was right on schedule; I had eclipsed the entire shoreline within a typical timeframe and without a hint or fair warning of what was about to transpire. I fancied myself a healthy individual, as healthy as I saw fit to live a relatively extended life without wishing I could erase years of self-abuse at the hands of drugs, fried food, and booze; surely my affinity for the elixir of red wine was no cause for alarm.

A small, growing pressure began to fill the sides of my head and I found myself mildly annoyed, as headaches rarely waste their time on me. I thought my inhalations needed deepening, my oxygen supply low, so I sucked in more and more with each breath, hoping to dissolve the stingy pains. The pain refused to budge, and I kept on, slicing the air with my strong trot. It would take more than that to slow me. And it did.

I was rudely nudged off my balance beam when my piston of a right hand (slightly out of my focus that was straight ahead yet visible with every step) appeared as a swelled blur before my chin, instead of a closed fist. The sweat which continued to surf over my eyes reminded me that this was not merely a fun filled activity, and that some mild irritation would accompany its duration. I attributed the misrepresentation of my hand to this stinging annoyance, and did not bother to think of it any further.

I'd like to mention that wrist bands are a peculiar item, and to this individual a trifle silly in appearance. This quirk in my vanity causes me, at the sight of them, to chuckle. Moreover, the thought of wearing them provokes a deterioration in the stronghold I possess over my masculinity. No excitable explanation follows this thread of thought, but it does explain why I use the back of my hand as a windshield wiper for my forehead. And as I did just so on this the first day of September, I was frightened to see myself wiping my face with an oversized foam hand one might find obnoxiously obstructing views in the cramped, peanut shell floored stands of a ballgame. It was of course my own hand, yet catastrophic in size.

Everything all at once was sucked astern. My chest ran for my back, my heart searched for my tail, and my escaping breath was terribly afraid of my mouth. My feet and legs lost all coordination as my run turned into a sidestepping fit of clumsiness. I danced for a good twenty yards while incoherent, shrill cries escaped my mouth. I held my hand out as far from my body as possible, afraid of what it might do to me. Shocked and frightened by its appearance, flashes of death, dismemberment, and emergency rooms played ping-pong in my head. Had I been stung? What did I eat? Was I drugged? I'm dying, that's it...this is how it feels!

Slowing down, I took cover by a friendly tree and put my hand under my sweat saturated shirt, trying to conceal its ugliness. I could not believe I was dying. What was going to happen next? Would my face swell and bubble and blood leak from my ears like excess jelly from a donut? Would I suffocate? Where's the white light?

My head churned the watery butter within and I leaned my otherwise strong body against the uncomfortable bark. Not that there is comfortable bark, but I like to imagine it is possible. One for hugging, and such. My eyelids stretched open to new lengths and I panned the park, looking for an answer, a cure, a camera of candid sorts playing a gag on me. I found nothing more than a busied and selfish community, oblivious to the man with the freakish hand in obvious distress.

Panic commanded my every instinct, and when I

removed my hand from my shirt, it shrank and swelled, then the other hand, in unison, two lungs breathing in tandem. I closed my eyes hard and shrunk down to my knees. Again, I put my hands into my shirt and tried to slow my breath, but I could not and, in fact, felt it climbing. A persistent dizziness that takes out the legs grabbed hold of me and I opened my eyes again, searching for the tree to hold onto, which I found, and noticed my hands were mine again. A bucket of cold sweat poured from my head down the back of my neck, cooling my fear in an instant. It looked as if death's arrival had been cancelled, and my breath slowed with relief. I thanked whatever phenomenon had removed the freakish swelling, or illusion, for I hadn't been sure what was real.

Vanity returned and I worried how the spastic rain dance I had gauchely choreographed would appear to others. Again I looked around, and wished to be home without delay. I picked up my jog and headed back from where I came, into a decent trot, replaying what had just happened. Should I see a doctor? Do I need medication? What if I *am* dying? I tried to reason with myself, which is a great deal like playing chess with oneself since you already know the other's next move.

As I approached the area of the knights and rooks I wondered what a hassle it must be to carry lawn chairs all the way down there every day, but figured for most it was the exercise of the day and just enough to keep their joints from rusting. Before the thought had dissipated I looked down as I wiped my brow again and thought my heart had actually escaped me, when the sight of my overdeveloped feet, each nearly a yard in length, passed strikingly on the pavement before my eyes. I shrieked, and my stride turned aimlessly towards the tables. I did not know whether to run faster or stop, so I tried crying out for help, hoping someone would know what to do. I imagined my feet being cut off, endless blood pouring out, and the sweat covering me grew to a boil, angst and death filling my head. I looked down again to find miniature versions of my feet now popping out of the toes, as if giving birth to a litter. I wanted to remove my sneakers and free the poison that had overtaken their insides, but fear kept me hurdling onward, the small crowd now aware of my impending arrival, my squalls through a dry cough asking them to stop, please make it stop, just before I collapsed a handful of feet from the tables.

"Just like Alice Cooper," Hannah quipped after I signaled with a nod the end of my story.

I laughed, a polite offering, unable to make the connection, and she nudged closer, the first scenario I envisioned the apparent victor. Before Hannah could turn up the heat, nausea's untimely return surfaced and I groaned, clutching an invisible handbag to my stomach. My host asked if I was alright and I advised her of the discomfort I had earlier and of it's untimely reversion. I thought about leaving, but the sensation faded quickly and I kindly asked for a glass of water, worried and unsure of what might happen next. I prayed to a god who had been kind to me thus far, and asked for the winds to stay down long enough to consummate the blessed union about to unfold. Hannah's scent tiptoed around my head and I could taste her skin on my dried lips. From the kitchen she called out:

"Vey, do you like kids?"

I did not dislike kids, but that was not what she asked. There were a list of tangibles I would need hole-punched before giving a definitive response. If she had asked me if I enjoyed traveling, I would have offered the same mixed response.

"Yeah, sure, I guess." It depends on what kids, or whose kids, what kind of kids were we talking about because some can be really mean and ugly. Unsure where she was going, I turned and hung my arm over the back of the sofa, my head facing her dark silhouette in the kitchen lit only by the dainty stove light.

"I just meant in general, because I have a favor to ask, and if you say no, I will be forced to hit you with this frying pan." She held up what appeared to be a skillet, retrieved from the rack of pots and pans that hung from the ceiling like a gang of rock climbers posing for a calendar spread. I laughed, thinking she had some spunk to her and that the night might prove to be a successful one after all.

"Sure, shoot. What can I do for you?"

"Will you help me have a baby?" Her shadow stricken, straight face suggested there was no joking in this inquiry.

Apparently my thirst was of no greater importance than this side-splitting moment of desperation.

"Will I what?" I waited and hoped for her laugh to both relieve and irritate me, but it did not come. She leaned across the counter holding up the pan, offering her sincerity.

"Will-you-help-me-have-a-baby? I have been looking for the right guy and my boyfriend can't make babies 'cause his fish can't swim upstream. You seem nice, educated, healthy. What do you say?"

The clay shaping my face tried to bend to show its look of surprise, and I searched the candlelit room, quickly trying to figure out what was going on. I asked the word "what" a couple of times out loud to no one, and shook my head, which then began to throb.

Melanie hadn't even mentioned having children more than once or twice in the five-plus years we tried each others bed sheets out, so what was this woman thinking inviting such horror to my face? This had to be the cruelest of jokes someone was putting me through. Perhaps under different circumstances I would have played along for a few minutes, curious where it would take me, but that moment was far from then.

"Boyfriend? What? Wait…no, I'm sorry, are you kidding me?"

"Does it look like I'm kidding!" she asked and hurled the pan in my direction, sending it soaring over my head and onto the floor beyond the coffee table holding our empty wine glasses.

"What the—" I was cut off by another flying projectile, my arms covering my head. When I looked up she fired yet another pan, a small sauce pan I thought, and it caught me on the forearm I offered as a shield. Without delay she continued to empty her weaponry and I decided it was time to go. Quickly up on my feet I headed for the door, yelling at her to stop, calling out her lunacy for the world to hear. The pans continued in my direction, but her long-range aim was poor, and I wondered just how much cookware one person could own and how necessary it was.

Before I could reach the door Hannah screamed out towards the hallway where her bed and bathroom were, and quickly looking back I saw the scar on her neck redden: "Richie, he don't want to, get out here, make him do it!" I heard the rustle of moving furniture, perhaps a chair and something closing, a drawer or cabinet, and then a door opened, dispensing a beast of a man hidden in the dark light. My legs became heavy, stuck in the morass which held me down.

I was only a handshake away from him when his face shone in the glow of the candles Hannah had lit. I couldn't believe someone had been waiting in the other room while this woman was pretending to seduce and be seduced! He was over six feet, and very hairy I noticed, the mop on his head ratty and cut lazily at the shoulders. Shaving or any form of grooming apparently hadn't been a strong consideration to this man and I wondered if the rest of his band was in the other room ready to back him up if he said the secret word. If they were, I wondered how strong their fish were, why they hadn't been recruited—and what the secret word was. The only thing missing was a wife beater tee-shirt. Perhaps he did not, or could not, read the memo. His lack of a shirt altogether more than made up for this missing prop.

I tucked these thoughts away for another time.

"Whoa whoa, whoa," I put my hand up towards him hoping he didn't crush it, or eat it, and said "I don't know what's going on here, but she invited me." I stared blinking red arrows at the seductress. "I didn't know about you, or any of this baby talk. Keep me out of it!" The words ga-ga goo-goo flashed across my minds eye and I doused it with disinfectant.

The overgrown tree stump looked me up and down and chewed on something that was too thick to be gum, without swallowing. "You sayin' you're not attracted to my girl here?" He held his arm out and she bounced over into his grasp while he watched me hungrily.

"No, I—" The mini skillet Hannah was holding struck me in the foot and I hoped it was the last of them. "What the fu—"

"You sayin' you don't want a piece of this when it's offered to you?"

"No, I'm saying I don't want any kids! She's very pretty, but I barely know her, it was onl—"

"Pretty? You callin' this pretty?" He slid his hand down her backside and slapped her to confirm the firmness her bottom held, not to mention his insular intelligence. "This is absolutely gorgeous man. Top choice. See, we can't have no babies, doctors say my guys are too strong for her little body, so we would need someone with normal fish. You got normal fish?"

Blown away by the absurdity of the moment, I thought quickly.

"For the record, I had a vasectomy years ago, so I can't even have children, even if I wanted to," I held my left hand up, the other still affixed to my stomach, "but thanks for thinking of me." I inched towards the door and the two of them looked at each other, their faces long and instigating. The freed animal pushed her away from him, acting as if she were contagious and had just transformed into a rabid dog.

"You knew he couldn't have no babies, and you brought him home anyway! You dirty whore!" Richie's remark was my cue to leave as quick as possible, and the lock and door obliged as I slipped out, the yelling of two very disturbed people playing in the background.

Hell would not end as I turned towards the elevator and noticed the hall had grown at least a half-mile long. The illusions which marked this disturbing day returned in new forms, and I quietly asked for their removal. Inside my head, my brain felt like tea in a cup on a cross-country train ride, swishing and swaying from side to side, splashing over the rim and onto the saucer. I walked regrettably slow, still afraid of followers, and saw both my hands and feet were different shapes, now not just bloated as before, but scissor-cropped pictures for a collage to be hung on a dormitory wall.

My mouth was dry with stale wine and crackers. I tried to steady my breath, which had quickly struck up and maintained a torrid pace, and took big steps to try to make up the ground. I could not stay there, so moving was my only option, as distorted and chaotic as it was. With one hand on the wall, I crept and lunged, and the elevator came quicker than expected. It had probably only been thirty feet from the door I exited, my giant steps proving effective against this ignus fatuus. I pressed the button firmly and closed my eyes, figuring that which I could not see could not hurt me. I had heard that idea somewhere and hoped it proved viable. Inside my eyelids I pictured the elevator doors opening to a hot cavernous watery fire, awaiting my descent to its torment.

Such exaggeration was not to be found when they did open, but instead an obnoxious bright light inside mocking my existence. Before entering I checked left and right to see the hall was now of normal length, it's freshly vacuumed floors with their leftover tracks, and the assuredness of many stories muffled behind each closed door. I entered and quickly pressed one final button with another foam hand, chills burrowing into my spine. It was not until the streets that I felt the tears coming.

3

I looked down at my watch: half past the midnight hour, and this was clearly not how I had hoped to start a new day. On the elevator ride down I kept telling myself that tomorrow was the day that I turned it all around, a new day, a new chance to get things right, to become the man I envisioned I should be, was born to be. It was already tomorrow and I knew I was on the clock.

For the majority of my adult life my existence had been one of situational control, calculated risk, selfishness, and unwavering greed. I am forty two years old, a year removed from this tale, and with these thoughts lingering above (see for yourself) it is hard not to feel a bit of time may have been wasted. Plus, my hair doesn't grow in the length, directions, or places it used to—contrary to my wishes. This is no surprise, but generally the hair-loss/knowledge ratio has some semblance to it, showing stable upward growth. And while mine most likely would reflect a similar trend, I feel as though the knowledge I had gained those years had been the stuff of comics, not of Confucius.

My role, though—whatever the hell it was—had been played for too long from a safe distance, and only in relation to the feeding of my own desires. I shared the quality which we find excusable in those who live at a disadvantage, be it by handicap or social plight or geographical misfortune. They think of themselves in the immediate time and place, and scarcely further because they do not know if there will be such a time. I thought of myself and looked for, in every situation, something that would better the grand cause— the cause of "me"— and all the while I threw pity upon myself, yet wanted no one else to do so, for I felt myself to be a valuable fleece which no one should see and dare think woven from poor fibers or weak hands.

Of course, I was, from time to time—as the winds of chance do scurry things a bit when they blow fiercely enough—reminded of the value in charity and the warmth that can be absorbed by its gift, although these gusts did tend to be fleeting motivations thanks to a devilish magnet hidden deep within myself that sought, and could detect, opportunity and instant gratification so accurately that the ideals of goodwill, and all it had to offer, found themselves buried beneath immovable boulders. But that was soon coming to an end.

The front door to the building I had just left closed without a sound, and the rest of the world before me decided to make up for its silence.

"Those aren't cars, are they?" I asked myself this, trying

to follow the streaks of white light and yellow-reds that shot past me. They had to be moving upwards of two hundred miles per hour, yet I knew it was not possible. Each flash of light stopped suddenly at the demand of the stop sign on the corner, transformed into a car or a taxi, then shot away to light speed without so much as a hello or goodbye.

I had to have been drugged.

I thought back to any opportunities one might have had to do so, but all the straws I drew were short. I had made my own breakfast, lunch, and dinner, and snacked on granola bars, bananas, and caramels. Someone could easily have injected them and I might not have seen the holes! Wait, wouldn't I taste something? Probably not, and this idea seemed to have a peg-leg of support, but when and why would someone come into my house and inject my granola bars? They could have easily tainted my water, or my milk, or—

I decided that I would throw out all of my food as soon as I got home...if I got home. I would also have to eat out, and reasoned I was long overdue anyhow, so that would be a nice treat.

The night sky and it's hidden drawings bore down on me, leaving me huddled with claustrophobia—a new sensation to me, one of many I would soon discover. The cars in passing continued their dangerous pace, the city around them unfettered by their recklessness. I had a long way to go, or so it seemed. The production involved in getting downstairs left me dreading a mini-walkathon back home, but it seemed inevitable. Hailing a cab was certainly out of the question, considering I could hardly discern one from a pink cement truck at the time, and driving was not an option either. I had taken the town car, not the bumper car so I decided that leaving my wheels for the night was an annoyance I would survive. Luckily these streets did not have meters, which meant no chance of being ticketed. More downtown they appeared, at a rate of a quarter every 10 minutes. It seemed every year the time increments grew smaller. First it was a half hour, then fifteen minutes, and ten. Before you knew it they would all have credit card machines on them to pay by the second.

I walked, trying to shake off the drama from upstairs and regain focus upon what I had to do to get home. My best guess had the distance I need to travel at about two and a half miles, and this was the good news. Walking was a common recreation there in my town, and as a form of transportation, since parking convenience was at a minimum. Two and a half miles. No sweat.

I made it as far as the next corner before my progress was halted by traffic. I tried not to focus on anything other than my feet and the immediate ground before me. Keeping my head down, a trick which seemed to be useful in dealing with my problem, I let the sounds of the night be my guide. The cars did not sound rocket charged—in fact sounding as they should, their rusty mufflers choking and coughing up continuous stream of filth—while nothing else, to my ears relief, seemed misplaced. Not even the man who approached me and waited patiently beside for the red light to allow our crossing.

"What a beautiful night, wouldn't you say?" His sweet, yet scratched voice told he was a smoker, and a polite one. "Hot as the Dickens, but beautiful!"

I was more than afraid to look up, thoughts of a sixty foot tall man equipped with a miniature head toying with my mind's stammering projector. I nodded and muttered my approval, maintaining my fix upon the curb and the weathered cigarette butt casually lying on its side taking a nap. His grey ensemble smudged and dripped in my peripheral. The sensation of these distortions was akin to a sober acid trip, or whatever the kids might be calling it in today's hacky-sack circles. I felt straight, yet I could not say the same for the objects that made up my landscape.

"You'll have to do better than that to convince me you agree! A groan and a nod can mean many a thing!"

Yes, I thought, it means leave me alone, and I offered up a quick laugh, an appeasement of little worth.

With his chin high in the air, this I could see peeking over, he continued: "Before long it will be morning, and what will you think of it then? Will you grunt in its birth, so that the first sound it hears is something so ambiguous? How shall the day know it has begun right?"

"What?" I asked, confused. "I don't—"

"Then don't! Do! Won't be long before a night like this is a distant memory," the man with the hoarse voice I had then guessed to be in his fifties said with rapid fire, "and we are all clamoring for the return of summer, dreading the cold nights that lie ahead." All of his sentences trailed up instead of off, each final word's pitch high as the kites. "But you are too busy in your own head to take the time to care for such things, when they have spent your lifetime, and mine, and longer, caring for you and everyone else you know of with their consistency!"

Afraid to come across as rude, I offered an anxious reply that I felt would bring closure to the idea and, fate willing, seal our exchange in timely fashion. "You got me, I should appreciate them more, thanks for pointing it out!" I feigned a smirk as a flurry of cars ignored our presence and blew by the curb in a burst of heat and light, the faded sound of their exhausts pipes lagging behind, trying to keep pace

How long was this light?

I was afraid to jaywalk, for obvious reasons, and had no pressing urge to encourage this odd fellow. As if convinced I would, however, pain from a nerve in the base of my neck dug with a screwdriver's torque up into my skull and prevented me from coming up with another cliché to spout out; I wasn't sure which would have hurt more. He began whispering to himself, but I chose not to hear the words as the cars slowed down and the light, cut from a yellow raincoat, turned its glow to red. I darted an arrow's path to the other side, not to be out done by the sure footed, eager pedestrian.

"Tell me, what do you know about time?" my shadow asked, now walking backwards and in front of me, his hands jammed into his scruffy coat which stopped abruptly at his knees.

"Time?" I truly was in no mood. "I don't have a lot of it...be careful!" I tried to put a hand out for whatever help it might do, but it didn't stop him from backing smack into the impoverished trash corral, bouncing off like it were made of rubber gloves.

"Time is something you cannot respect enough—its value, its immeasurable nature!" He spoke with his hands, their zany movements hardly matching the words coming out or the black hat sitting atop his head.

"Immeasurable?" Seconds, minutes, hours, days. Next theory, please.

"In terms of its preciousness, I say! You cannot harm it, for to do so is a crime!" He pumped his fist several times into the air, as if celebrating a victory.

"Ah yes, not enough hours in the day, I hear you."

"Do you know why the pudding's rat race is never on ice?" He asked this as though the answer would astound me.

"Do I know why the pudd—"

"No you don't, because neither do I!" He froze in his steps as this seemingly wonderful thought washed over him; my feet never stopped.

"Take care!" I said aloud with the quick raise of my hand, and scurried across another sun bleached crosswalk, the traffic lights in my favor. I generally enjoyed the small talk, even the absurd, yet this man had chosen the wrong night to try to engage me.

It is a funny thing, weather chat, and one which eclipses all cultures. Anyone can talk about the weather: It's hot, it's cold, it's cloudy, it's sunny. It is a common thread we all share in our everyday lives. So since we know this, not a day goes by in which one cannot retrieve a quip from their pocket on the status of the sky and offer it up with confidence and in turn receive an equally unoriginal thought to complement it. I personally try to take these opportunities to make some poetic statement on the precariousness of life and the current state of society's affairs. I say things like: (upon hearing a sad note on the rain) "I like to think of it as a cool, relaxing shower after the world's dirty day of work." Some people nod and say things back like "Damned if you do, damned if you don't" or "You can't win 'em all".

This gentleman surely would have welcomed my thoughts and there initially appeared the potential to share a slice of wisdom shortbread until he decided to reveal his footsie pajamas. Off his rocker, the man was full of splinters and I hoped he didn't recognize me, a self-serving concern I often had, yet I was sure he would have asked if I were the "Painter Guy" by then, as I was often referred. Not that I was by any means a celebrity in this city, but yes, many of my works hung in some principal buildings and penthouses here and there in the miles nearby, and I made the papers on occasion, while my annual New Year's shows have created some buzz; yet I wouldn't say my name was a household one. Besides, there were other artists of sorts and people of stature whose names were a great deal more recognizable than my own sharing my zip code. And how talented was I? I didn't even have the dexterity to build my own frames, a Lincoln Log experiment gone bad, and my yearly exhibit was held in a pricy art store owned by one of my aunt's friends. Still, I suppose, there were times when I was commended, or called out, or asked for an autograph. If only they knew what worthlessness my illegible scribble actually held! So I grappled with the reality of my own success

Keeping my head down, I trudged on. This course of action continued to work, and I covered substantial ground without taking note of unnecessary distractions. The section of the city where Hannah had lived was dotted with bars, restaurants, and convenience stores, so I knew traffic to be heavier there as I neared the midnight hour, yet after a good ten or twelve blocks away the quiet of the night took over and the sounds of hushed romances and liquored pedestrians reminded the city it was not alone.

The summer nights there are pleasant ones, a constant buzz humming in the background of the streets, a surprise party waiting to happen. Down by the water and out of my sight, the lights which lit the park sparkled in their solace and reassured the calm which slept in the safety of its grass. The smell of the water, it's swaying sounds echoing in the tall trees, was an inviting one of safety and purity, well aware of the a tug-o-war it would soon play with the freshly baked bread and muffins of the new morning.

Crime's toll was minimal, with the exception of the occasional car theft or vandalism any town plays victim to. The people, it seemed, were void of the character necessary to perpetrate violations against one another, each trying to construct a quilt of decency in which to wrap themselves in. I had never heard of a murder in the city, although fifteen years back an elderly woman was accused of poisoning her husband to death with antifreeze in his coffee. It later was found that the senile man had poisoned himself every morning, thinking the antifreeze to be alcohol, and spiked his own joe daily without telling his wife. Fingerprints covering the bottle—and his casual mention of this to the proprietor of a local coffee shop—had freed the poor woman of any wrongdoing. Before the first bites of lunch were taken the next day I would play a significant role part in ending this drought.

For a moment I lost track of my whereabouts and dared peek at my surroundings. Still moving steadily, I looked to see many a thing: I saw the misshapen forms of lampposts, bent halfway up and curved over with the ease of warm taffy; I saw apartment buildings and storefronts whose facades rose up infinitely to kiss the clouds hidden in the dark haze of the sky; I saw mailboxes stuffed with other mailboxes; I saw tiny cars and giant cars and puddles of cars too; I saw a cab move steadily past me, to my left and then stop as if there were a cliff ahead, then back up slowly and stop within a few feet away from me. The cab was a standard yellow one, and I was relieved at the normalcy of it, until out from the rear door popped the man I would shortly be accused of murdering.

"Hey there," he called out to me, louder than necessary, his overwhelming attire of gray to match his shoes catching me by surprise. Into his pocket he delved and summoned a crisp bill to pay the driver. I stopped, hoping to bring some finality to our acquaintance, and awaited his story. The sight of his arm extending through the driver's chest and into the oncoming lane of traffic alarmed me, and I took a couple of casual steps back, hoping I would not meet the same curious fate as the driver who then sped off, unharmed.

He smiled, showing thousands of teeth and I decided I had had enough of the trick and pony show. I closed my eyes firmly, opening them carefully, hoping to erase the scene. Sweat seeped down my temples, my collared shirt clinging to my damp back. Inside my pants, mold would surely have formed if the heat and moisture did not escape at some point. I imagined a mushroom garden growing out of the cuffs.

"I apologize for bothering you! Wait, did I say you? Me? Who's bothering who here, for I am just as inconvenienced! Some might call that bothersome. Agreed!"

Again he reached into his pocket and this time retrieved a black mass of some sort, offering it up to me. "Is this yours? You dropped it a while back." He held out my misshapen wallet and the sour milk in my stomach curdled.

A car shone past without time to breathe and I saw the night growing longer than I had wished. I reached out and took my wallet, opening it to read the letters that made out my name, occupation, mailing address, phone number, and e-mail address stamped on my business card.

"Yeah that's me, thanks!" I held it up to him and shook it, convinced he had opened it, unsure if he took any money. I didn't care either way. "I can't thank you enough, maybe some day I'll return the favor." I could not believe the words that left my mouth. The invisible fist I possessed punched me in the right side and I cursed myself to the heavens. I smiled, blinked twice, and turned towards my destination, picking up a modest trot.

My new friend followed my lead and kept pace beside me.

"Do you believe that a penny saved is a penny earned?" he asked, as happy as could be.

"That's what they say." Well, someone did.

"*They*? Oh son, *they* are of you just as much as you are of *they*. Do not exclude yourself and think that referring to them as *they* will provide you with a defection from them just because you refer to them as such!" His words continued to float up. "I do not chide myself with such naïve thoughts, and that is why I am not *they,* but you sir most certainly are!"

"O-*kay*..." I said, trailing off.

"Again you spit on time as if it were recyclable, in surplus, not worth a feather." His cotton, brimmed hat was now yellow; I knew it to be black moments before. "Tell me, how many seconds can you put into a bowl of soup? Well, add five to the number of ones on a clock and throw in a pair of twos and add two!"

Stop. Please Stop. I felt I deserved at least that much. Simply for this man to stop talking to me was all that I asked! Once home I would try to sleep off the discrepancies that haunted my waking moments, but until then I could not listen to any more of this silliness. It was as if he knew of my inexorable pain, and was sent to add to it.

"Look, I don't know where you're going with this, but I really am in a hurry and I doubt you're going as far as I am." I had had enough.

"I am not a follower, my petticoat does not suit that function, I but only a messenger of truth and I hope you will take heed to my fair warnings. A fly in the pie means goodbye!"

I laughed out with a jerk of my head and turned it into polite cough, then nodded again, saying not a word, hoping my silence spoke volumes.

"You sir, are a blind man!" he said. "So how much shall you pay for the wind's cooperation?"

Again I stifled the urge to laugh, my begrudging resolve strong as the proverbial bull.

"Very well then, I leave you, a scamp of a man, with the bowl void of it's count and a pleasant evening!"

I was hopeful his farewell toast was sincere, yet he kept pace and I assumed his newfound silence was only temporary. His hat quietly changed colors numerous times and several blocks passed before he began humming a scattered tune with only two notes. Apparently his goodbye was not goodbye. I could no longer tolerate the anguish my head was serving up. I had never imagined that such simplistic, polite notations on the weather could evoke murderous caprice in my head, but there I was. If equipped with a knife or other obvious weapon I most assuredly would have offered it to him unkindly, regardless of his immediate regard for me. I wanted to tell him to go away, come on back another day, and he left me with one last question, although in the moment I thought his barrage of lunacy would ring eternal.

"Have you answered it?"

"Answered what?"

"I think you know."

"If I do, are we finished?"

"I would say the business at hand shall then be decided!"

"Sixteen," I said, and was stopped dead in my tracks when a passing car backfired twice and I flinched, holding my hands to the side of my head to keep its contents from spilling out. To my good fortune, they did not, but a steady pain-filled peal filled its walls and echoed, picking up speed with each revolution. I cried out to the otherwise tranquil night, trying to stagger on. I no longer heard the voice that had encouraged my growing rage, and assumed he was scared off, or put off by my rudeness. Or that I had solved the riddle and he had honored our agreement. I was mildly relieved, now only concerned with not dying on a street corner, alone and afraid.

From that point it became a test of my equilibrium and determination. Every inch of my flesh asked to collapse in a heap, for it had grown tired of the confusing walk I was carrying it through. I ignored these persistent requests, and before long, without managing any further harm to myself or others, found myself inside the dark and quiet foyer of my townhouse—ashen, crying, aching, and surprisingly hungry.

The word home may elicit different meanings do different folk, yet the common denominator in all their ideas, if you were to delve, would be the sensation of a safe haven, a place where one is always welcome. On this night, home felt akin to a mother's womb, a kangaroo's pouch, or the inside of a Midwestern shelter below a torrid tornado. I flicked the wall switch by the door, and awakened the glamorous chandelier I once coveted dearly. Why the hell did I have a chandelier? What was the point of it, and who was I impressing? I was suddenly disgusted with myself, and admitted that all of this was undoubtedly payback of sorts for years of misbehavior.

I waited for the cylindrical shaped lobby to begin spinning and surprise me with its doubling as a carnival gravity ride. It did no such thing, but the paintings that hung on its curved walls glared at me, sneering and shaking their heads with disapproval.

I slunk down to the floor and brought my knees to my chest, closing my eyes. I was overcome with dysphoria. Regret for all the wrong I had ever done and all the hearts I had broken and all the lies I had told myself, or otherwise. I was a forlorn captive, abandoned, whipped from the cane of a thousand untruths, across my cowering back. I sobbed, an incoherent mess for a minute or two and used my shirt to dry my face to a reddened polish. I sniffed the remaining tears away as the pain and stomach discomfort evaporated too.

After a couple of minutes I opened my eyes to find myself at home, washed out, and symptom free. Several promises were quickly made at that moment, promises to make better choices, to eat more vegetables, and to help the elderly cross the street. The art above me continued its scowl, knowing these to be empty promises, ones I had made before, ones I would forget by next morning. I tried to lie and tell them this time was different, but they knew me too well.

The first piece I had ever sold, the oil painting platter of cocktail shrimp coffins, hung quietly and unassuming, and led me to believe there was one in the group that still had hope for me. I had aptly named it the Wheel of Misfortune, at age twelve, its debut being at my middle school's year-end festival. Looking up at it with nostalgic eyes, I let them well up again as I played back the day we learned of my good fortune. The day is not exactly what leaves an imprint, but the ensuing night, when we celebrated. I had worn my first suit, and felt like a king; I felt important; I felt tall; I felt like somebody. The "we" in all of this being my parents and myself.

The mayor of the city, at the time, had offered my folks five hundred dollars for the painting, a rather morbid display of blacks and reds. The mayor had struck me as a rather gloomy fellow himself, so it was not surprising he coveted the piece. The young people of the city had called him "Count Dracula," because of his striking resemblance to Stoker's legend. It wasn't until years later that I would learn, upon his death, that the reference was not all that far fetched.

His family, and later anyone with keen interest, would discover that the basement of his home had been transformed into a modern day dungeon. Two barred cells equipped with beds and high mounted shackles for genuine effect highlighted the very dark, open room that was once used for folding laundry and storing winter clothes. While some men transformed their basements into sports bars, the mayor had his built to torture and imprison. No proof of such wrongdoing was ever shown or proven, and his wife said he only went down there when he had a hard time sleeping. I hadn't heard of a coffin turning up.

My painting apparently fit the motif quite comfortably, and hung there until his widow later auctioned off most of his play toys, which included a life sized skeleton, a collection of iron torches, medieval replicas of weapons, and a bunch of other stuff I didn't have, never would, and didn't care about. Except for one.

It was at this very auction that I seized the opportunity to reclaim the painting that would start it all, the dusty piece with the initials "VA"—with the left side of the A woven into the V as if it were one letter—in the lower right corner, reclaimed for the small sum of fifty dollars.

My parents were embarrassed by the five hundred dollar offer he had made us so many years back, claiming it "far too much for a middle school art exhibit," and asking "What would the other parents think?" Mayor Dracula was most insistent, advising them he would admit to only having paid one hundred dollars, then upped his minimum and final and offer to one thousand, almost all of which ended up in my first-ever savings account; there was the matter of a suit. I had just turned twelve two weeks before that night and we dressed formally, the navy suit I bought with my own money—and clip on tie I was so proud of—signifying the night's importance, complementing the endless smile I wore with it throughout dinner and the rest of the night.

Three decades later I continued to stare at the work, framed in a thick, ebony square, while I tasted new, warm tears which spoke of my love for my mother and father. I missed them terribly, and hoped they knew how much I adored them and appreciated all they did for me.

Surely they could both play the harp by now and I could hear their songs as they massaged my heart. There, as I held myself and swayed to the strings, I slinked to the floor, a welcome mat and the weight of the earth below me, and slept.

4

It was clear I was wanted for murder. Not when the police came to the door, knuckles and carpus blazing, but once into my breakfast it became blatantly obvious.

Deprived of formal police training, I could not be completely convinced what constituted substantial evidence, yet I could assume that video surveillance of myself and the victim moments before his death did not bide well for me. The moment I saw the watered down, black and white clip that showed the two of us walking together—I with my head down and stumbling drunk or otherwise—I knew this day would not improve upon the last. I also knew that the backfires I had heard were anything but.

The rapping on the door which I slept against shook fear to my core and woke my defense with taut chills. The strained look on my face held shape while I studied the bright foyer for alterations.

I decided never to sleep there again.

A second round of knocks quickly stuck the door. I was

hardly amused and crawled slowly away, my head heavy with the faint screams of a waking dinosaur echoing inside. I hardly got a yard away and my newly mobile corpse stiffly crept up towards the peek hole to find whose nerve dared to be so crass, and before I could reach it, the knell of my doorbell sent tones of shrapnel hurdling off the walls of my foyer. As I stifled the urge to voice my disapproval, the officers vocalized their identities and claimed to possess a couple of questions for me.

I deduced that Hannah had done something vengeful I would have to deal with, and I was in no mood; I decided to eat and shower before dealing with any of it.

I mechanically and quietly shrank back to the floor, looking like a silent horror film villain, and held my breath. Knocking again—softer this time—they grumbled something unintelligible while one of their radios chirped, commanding my attention and demanding that I take heed. My ear to the cold, oak door, hesitant seconds passed and I heard them get back into and drive away in their cruiser, my heart earnestly jumping rope the whole time.

A mélange of scooped cereal and milk pleasured my mouth while I clicked the television on, hoping for background noise or moving pictures to detract my worries. The morning news opened with a diluted clip of someone walking down Riverside Avenue, described as a "person of interest," alongside a man dressed entirely in gray who had been gunned down shortly thereafter, blocks away on an ill-lit crosswalk. This person's identity—the alleged gunman—was unknown, but the still lingering rasps from my front door told otherwise.

No, I tried to convince myself, this can't be. After all I had endured the night before, it had come to this? Murder? I was dreaming, that's all there was to it.

Bemused by their antics, I searched the confines of logic to offer an explanation to the officers' seemingly indifferent visit. If confidently secure in their scrutiny of the situation, and I as their prime suspect, then the half-hearted effort to apprehend me stood as a less than comforting representation of the city's finest. It was conceivable that their presence was in fact to secure information regarding a certain painter's keyed car, or a stolen candlestick from Hannah's apartment, and I offered the gods whatever restitution they sought fair to make it so.

Unimpressed by my newfound faith, they replied without a sound, referring me to the coverage that continued in the animated box.

I refrained from wasted sophistry, as I was advised that the police had discovered further tragedy in a fifth floor condo a mile from the man in gray's bullet riddled corpse, the strangled body of a thirty-six year old liquor store clerk named Hannah Valenti. Ms. Valenti's (irascible by my account) boyfriend, Richard Mansucci, a thirty-eight year old electric company technician, had returned home after a night of partying to find her beaten and strangled. Her supposed meeting with a well-known local artist, Veymont Addison (regarding art for their new condo), apparently took a terrible turn as their home was found upturned, along with a wine glass securing the assailant's fingerprints, and a damning writing sample in the form of a television guide crossword.

A scamp of a man? Was I?

The walk home had been grated in so many places as I feverishly tried to replay it over and over again, in reverse, upside down, in and out. I wondered if I had actually killed these innocent people: the man in gray pushing me to my social limits, and Hannah unabashedly asking of me what no woman has dreamed ask before.

Was I even capable of such leonine violence? Where would I have gotten a gun, and where was it now? And what about Hannah? Had I actually strangled her? I wished for answers in a penniless fountain.

The symptoms which crippled me the day before had not returned, luckily, for I knew my reaction to them would help inlay the tiles of my alleged crimes and toss me into the mudded gulch. I plead for their seclusion while driving to turn myself in, freshly showered and well fed, expecting neither luxury upon my arrival.

My face dredged with anxiety, I extended an apology for not answering the door earlier and this struck them with marked appreciation and scold. Without a search warrant (another oddity I pondered), they refrained from using force to locate and apprehend me, and assumed I had fled due to the absence of any vehicles in my drive. Not because—as I had imagined—I was a genial fellow with honorable intentions.

Tedious days of waterless labor seemed to pass as I waited and melted in my shattered dreams and torment, not sure of anything anymore, the voices all making too much sense and not enough all together in disarray. I glanced up at the clock, crooked on the metal-green painted cement wall and wondered how long the jail hold would last. I had been there for nearly two hours, fearing what twenty to life would feel like, when the locked door opened with tired rust, and in stepped my lawyer, looking unpleased, which pained me, for I longed to please her.

“Hello, Angel. Caught stealing brushes again?” My focus should have been on the circumstances that cued this encounter, on her obliging arrival, at the severity of my detainment, yet all I could think of was how much I wanted to nibble on her legs. They tempted me in such a way as to make the incarceration worthwhile.

“Mel,” I wanted to offer up an excuse, but hadn’t the appetite for my own cooking, “I’m sorry.” Time was precious, and a life dangled over a gloss of salivated incisors. My money was no good, and as far as she was concerned, I probably was too. “I don’t even—”

“Save it, just tell me what the hell I’m doing here.” Her demanding tone excited me. “And why you never killed me when you had the chance, because I’m sure you thought it once or twice." I welcomed the sarcasm, thankful she held the spit pail in my corner.

"Every night I tried, but just couldn't bring myself to do it Melanie. I loved your cooking!" The reciprocity of our smiles and the sight of her white, white teeth reminded me why I had once considered meeting her at the end of the aisle.

She proceeded to tell of the obstacles we were faced with and the grim possibility of a quick exit. Along with the glass which would eventually prove my lips to have drunk from, were hairs (short, gray ones from my head, I deduced), a writing sample from her skillfully filled in television guide crossword, and eyewitness testimony of the noise and screams heard from the adjoining units. In addition, I was held in the murder of Samuel Cheshire, the man in gray, after video showed the two of us walking together one block from where he was killed, along with my business card in his coat pocket.

He took a business card? I wondered what I had gotten myself into.

"Angel, what have you gotten yourself into?" she asked, her eyes pleading with me to explain this was all a gross misunderstanding and that I had a newfound affinity for cream cheese. She never could accept the fact that I disliked the spread, preferring jam on my bagels. I never thought it an issue, yet every time I passed up on the dairy delight, she shook her head in disgust, as if I had just hid unpleasant food under the table in my napkin.

I openly admitted the strangeness the day had taken on, from the park to the baby donation drive to the man I saw on the news splattered on the crosswalk. I had given the officers the same version, or the one I believed to be true—minus the unlikely details of my eye affliction—and they seemed unimpressed. Melanie knew me better than most, the residual effect of the on-again off-again relationship we weathered for the better part of five years. She knew when I was bending the truth, and her relaxed posture indicated her belief. She warned me not to deceive her in the slightest or I would find myself looking for another savior, one I would not enjoy undressing with my eyes. The stress of her threat reminded me of the last thing she said to me when we parted ways, several years now passed:

"You will always be alone, and never be happy, because you never let anyone in, and all you care about is yourself!" I often saw a few of the words, as if she were writing them, in her handwriting behind my eyelids... *"never be happy..."*

The words vexed me for years, their scratches leaving marks whenever I summoned them.

"When did this begin? The mushroom trip?" she asked, pulling back a chair. She dropped her purse onto the table which separated us, then sat and slid in, hiding her crossed legs from me. I wondered if lawyers had done away with briefcases in favor of designer hand bags—a wonder I would keep to myself.

"Yesterday, that was the first time. It was like no drug I've ever tried!" She looked at me with doubtful eyes. "Okay, well not exactly," I said, remembering who I was speaking to.

I will not bore you with tales of talking monkeys or being chased from a trailer by a man with a shotgun, nor will I waste your time with stories involving a knife-wielding cab driver threatening me for a tip or accidentally kidnapping a clown, yet these are all truths Melanie knew to be just. My life at that moment, suddenly a much more serious one than in years past, seemed to depend upon the recollection of more pressing details, and alibis I could procure, so ghost stories of my wilder days can certainly wait.

Together we assimilated a shotgun defense, and she promised to do all she could to expedite my release. I had offered up a paltry helping of details, the haze of the evening tainting the memories with doubt and bewilderment. The happenstance of the crimes—I knew were not of my hands, deformed or otherwise—was damning, yet without a murder weapon, motive, or conclusive witness to either, we were confident of my vindication.

Melanie left without a good-bye kiss, one I could have greatly used. I could not determine with any certainty whether the cold front she put forth was an effort to try to prove her emigration from my hold, or if the business at hand had eclipsed any notions of our gravitation. I desperately wanted to ask her if she was seeing someone, but couldn't find the proper opening during her tedious questioning. It was near impossible to be in her vicinity without the reminder of how electric we were together. The chemistry we shared was obvious, even in the dimly lit holding room. I wanted to crawl across the table and drag her on top of it with me, the jumpstart of a small spaced, lip-and-body wrestling match to be held three feet off the ground.

I studied her lips as she spoke and hoped they would not find their way to another's when she left. Had I blown my chance? No, there was always a chance for us, even she had admitted that. I played back a distant, lasting moment when she had said that if in twenty years time I called upon her and asked her to be mine, she would lose the ensuing struggle to decline the offer. I possessed that great of a fix on her.

I wondered if fear had evoked these thoughts in me, fear of being jailed infinitely, fear of losing out on my chance at love, fear of never touching a woman's flesh again. Inside my head, a book began to fill with worries and regrets. I shelved the work in progress and decided that thinking the matter into submission would not prove to be a successful endeavor. I would revisit the thoughts in the morning and see what a new dawn might bring.

My first night in a jail cell came equipped with the overwhelming smell of feet and stale water. I thought I smelled a vanilla candle nearby, but it must have been my imagination. Maybe the head jailer, or whatever he was called, had lit a candle to set the mood. I pretended it so. The rest of the night proved uneventful, and I was ignored, for the most part, except for the undercooked microwave dinner escorted to my cell unassumingly, made up of refurbished chicken, watery corn and a mass whose concept I believed to be mashed potatoes. It was the worst thing I had ever eaten, and I wondered if prison food tasted half as good.

Morning came as scheduled, never late as I sometimes wish. Also right on time was my release, Melanie on hand to absorb the look of relief that scarred my face, and also most likely to welcome the heaping of gratitude I would surely cast upon her.

I wished to retract the thanks I offered her, when, outside in the warm September morning, the sky's ceiling having taken on new heights, she told me that video and eye witness evidence had filtered in the evening before exonerating me on both counts, and that she had used her charm to keep me hostage for the night, playful vengeance as her motivation. I flipped.

"What? Are you kidding me? After the day I had, you thought I deserved that!" I wanted to deface, in vulgar fashion, the smirk she wore on her pretty face, but quickly realized it was overdue payback on a very personal level. Time served. I shut my mouth.

Apparently the body of Ms. Valenti had only been dead

for under two hours when it was reported at dawn, and the video footage from her building's lobby showed my arrival and exit just as I had said, while never showing either for Mr. Mansucci throughout the night. My recorded stroll with the man in gray shortly after midnight did not hurt either. In that matter, the bullets found at the crime scene matched those from a gun found in a speeding car two towns over, shortly after the estimated time of Mr. Cheshire's death. Oops.

Melanie, too, remained silent, and I rejoined her in stride as we walked to her car.

"Thank you," I said humbly. "For whatever you did Or didn't do...thanks. I owe you."

"You bet your sweet ass you do!" Melanie grinned and eternity dimmed briefly trying to regain it's breath. "Someday I might actually collect."

The ride was hushed, our lips stuck shut, the radio thoughtfully saving us from the exposition of one another's thoughts. My attraction to her was stronger than ever, and I lazily combed my eyes down her several times, slowing as the picture faded. I could not resist as I realized that twenty years from now she would still have a hold of *me.* I had seen the potential end of my freedom playing out before me—a distinct possibility at the time—and in the hours before my release I was thinking my life had been well-rounded, a pleasure filled adventure, and one of much love; I decided I had no regrets. I had curled up in this thought, warm and snug, justifying my existence and the sunsets I let pass. Melanie walked into the room and I caught a raindrop which told I actually did have *one* regret. She tagged me Angel when she saw me, but she was in fact the true angel, come to save, bearing smiles and hopes. I feared that night she would find her lips touching those of another, her love shifted to him and slipping away from my pull. What if she were to return home to find her new love bent on a sturdy knee, asking for her hand?

I often displayed exigent panic and sought swift resolution to my fears. Now was not the time. My need to profess my thoughts, expose my fears, carve out the worry, and swallow the entrails would have to wait. The exodus from incarceration certainly was not the sexiest of times, and I decided that that night I would perform a chivalrous act, a suicide from habit, one that showed I could love in ways foreign to my creed, the way she knew I could, and ultimately wanted to.

The engine slowed, sighed, and then hummed steadily as we sat in Melanie's car, yards from my own which I had left on a downtown side street two nights before. Somehow it had made its way back to my house and I had no recollection of the move. Mel later informed me the police had swiftly located and impounded the car for any evidence it might hold, and after my innocence was found they used the keys I had handed over at my unexpected surrender to return it to my street, as a courtesy for the inconvenience they had caused. They were even courteous enough to leave fingerprint dust on the door handles and steering wheel! So thoughtful.

I put my hand on her arm, gently, lovingly. "I owe you my deepest gratitude." I said. "Truly, Mel, thank you again. Let me take you to dinner, tonight, really show my thanks." I smiled and began caressing her arm, to show my thoughts were removed from self-service, but looking back it had the opposite effect. Her face now distressed, she frowned, her squinted eyes mocking me. I couldn't be sure if it was genuine or for effect as frowns are rarely so pronounced, but it appeared as though the sides of her lips were dripping wax.

"I don't know, Vey." Her compressed forehead asked me not to toy with her any longer, and I understood, smiling soft and warm.

"I know, dear, I know. Let's talk, I'm not who you think I am." I was of course just having a relapse from myself. Melanie knew it and exploded.

"Oh and who are you then, Veymont? Wait, let me guess, Veymont isn't your real name, it's an alien name! Are you from the planet Veymont? Is that it, is that why you *just can't help yourself* Vey? Huh? Is that it? What the hell kind of a name is Veymont anyway?" It was French, she knew this. Old material. "Gee, no wonder you're so confused all the time, your own name doesn't even make any sense!" She looked out her window, and kept her head turned away from my view.

Her flak cut open sores and the volume quickly turned

down, the cloud cover above thickening, threatening. I tasted sulfur and fire, and swallowed hard. I deserved the lashing, perhaps a great deal more, even. She needed to understand who I really was, but even I didn't know, and twenty two and a half hours under lock and key was by no means the schooling I needed.

"I've changed, Mel. Honestly."

"Since when?" She whipped back around. She would have put her hands on her hips if she were standing, a pose I was familiar with. "Since when Veymont? Since being detained and having a sleepover in jail ?" I was actually arrested, not just detained, but there was no active tally in progress.

"Yeah, actually. Yes." I quickly realized I had to give more and shook my head. "And no...before that! I'll explain. Just have dinner with me later, so we can talk." I softened my excited tone." If you don't like who I am, you can double my fees." I locked eyes with her and gave a tug.

I could feel her tongue licking the back of her teeth. It wasn't apparent to watch her, but she did so when trying to decide something. Her cheeks rose and widened, a resistant smile escaped, and she shook her head. "Just to talk, and you better remember I have the power to put you behind bars." I told myself she really didn't. Sure, she could keep me behind bars which I was already behind for short and unnecessary periods of time, but no, not put me there. I was splitting fibers, again lacking an operational tally.

“Thank you.” I said, flashing an earnest smile.

“Don’t thank me yet. I haven’t done anything, and I don’t know if I want to.” I told myself she did.

We exchanged a warm hug, and part of me felt renewed. I noted how fragile my emotions were, how the simplest of gestures could set me soaring above the lampposts and the trees.

And how just as quickly I could dismiss the same feelings altogether.

As our embrace untangled, I felt sorry for exciting her heart and cursed myself. I realized I had wanting nothing more from her and for her to not love me any longer. I understood that it was the capture of a heart that I desired, not the culmination of years of shared experience and attraction. I wasn’t afraid of being in love, for I enjoyed the fever of loving, the soup that came with it only increasing my temperature. Loving was never the problem, while ultimately being the only problem. I loved to be in love. Over and again.

I closed the door, and after she pulled away her stare held me awkwardly and uncomfortably tight. She drove off, paying no mind to the box truck barreling hard down the road whose roof hung with overgrown trees, shadow kaleidoscopes flickering behind in the breeze.

Within seconds the horrific entanglement of steel and flesh marked the end of a life. It was the first time I had been witness to an accident of such magnitude, such absolute catastrophe, the martyr of chance playing such a nasty hand, and I had to wonder if a bit of tomfoolery was involved. With a skeptical eye I checked my cards and folded.

5

Death had decided to shadow me, or it truly and regrettably possessed poor aim. Either end, to be near me was an obvious danger; possibly it was time to get away from myself. It wouldn't be long before my own death flashed across the front page of the papers, headlines sounding the end of the strangest of chapters our unassuming little city had ever played host to. The thought of impending demise failed to escape me while I sat on my stoop, my left palm supporting my chin, the right on a cold, shaking back.

"You okay?" I asked, knowing the unlikelihood of my inquiry.

"Yeah, I guess. I just can't believe that happened." Melanie's face was frozen with shock, the black ensemble she wore befitting the scene. "I can't believe he didn't take me with him."

"I know..."

"That poor, innocent man is gone. All because of me. If I hadn—"

"Don't, Mel, that's not fair. You couldn't see him...he was flying! He never should have been going that fast."

I looked down at my hands, at the lines in the palms, and I saw that some ran long and thick, while others — and these I feared— were cut short and faded. What did these dried out rivers indicate my fate was? I did not want to know.

I felt responsible for the mess, for what Melanie must be feeling, and what she would be feeling once I revealed my self again to be nothing resembling what I had hoped to profess. I felt ashamed for being at the heart of so much hurt and heartache in the world all at once. But to acknowledge such fault and take responsibility for my actions, I would be forced to admit the slight of my hand, if you will, or my evil tongue and its bullet-piercing lashings. I refused to shame myself, again thinking only of myself and how weak I might appear.

I closed my eyes and saw Melanie's words, *"all you think about..."* She was right. And at the rate I was going I would never be happy.

My little one-man-band of seduction knew its performance moments before was a solid one, and left her understandably distracted when she pulled out. A quick glance in the side mirror would have warned her of the large white mass hurdling down my street well above the posted speed limit. Fast I will grant, but nothing outrageous from my observation. In my memory I tried to, but could not, recall ever driving down a street under, or even at, the posted speed limit, so I was the last person to be blaming speed on anyone. Plus, my foot, which some claim to be made from a mold composed entirely of lead, was not one that would idly stand by and allow me to voice such accusations.

Truth be told, I admired the reflexes he showed, veering to his left to avoid her shiny black jeep, but not the end result. I couldn't imagine box trucks ever being known for their handling, and all sixteen feet of its load, plus the cab, proved just why when it skimmed the row of cars opposite where I sat, flipping with the ease of a greased pancake. The driver cut left, than back, but the quick swerve spun him like a mid-air quarter. The weight of the truck sat on my conscious, and I continued to stare out into the street and curse my selfish mouth for acting once again without a clue of its power.

"Were you really going to call me tonight, or was this just the *crest* of another one of your *waves* of emotion?" Melanie's tone was filled with sarcasm, pity, and indifference.

"I don't know...it's hard to see you and not be reminded of how good we can be." My sight remained locked on the strewn remains of the calamity which would surely play encore snippets in my head in the days and months to come. I had become a collector of disasters, and it was now common practice to find them without trying.

"It's okay, Vey, I didn't believe you, anyway. When I turned the key I was thinking that you were just following your ever-indecisive heart, and that within ten minutes you would be second guessing your efforts to charm me."

"Really? Am I that transparent?" She was a liar if she said no and I knew it.

"You kinda are, I'm sorry. I wasn't upset, I've learned to accept who you are. I still love ya, but I can't trust your heart for the life of me. And I wasn't planning on it."

"I'm sorry Mel, I guess I'm really no good for anyone."

"Oh don't pull that self deprecating crap, you're not getting any sympathy here. You know what you need to do."

"Do I?"

"I think you do." She took a deep breath and sighed, looking down. She bunched her lips to make a face that said she felt sorry for me. "But maybe you just can't see it yet. Those walls you hide behind aren't as transparent."

"Maybe we could spend some time together and you could help show me?" I was sincerely hoping she would take me up on the offer. I felt this moment was somehow portent.

"I don't think so, Vey, I can't put myself through that anymore. What you need, I can't give you."

"And what is that?"

"A new set of eyes."

I was a prisoner of my own defense and I accepted the shackles, for it was my own doing, depths surely unknown to those of admirable munificence or immortalized in stone. She had predicted it a long time ago, a simple prognosis of eternal dismay caused by the lack of my ability to trust the one thing I guarded most.

Unsure of exactly what had me reassessing my life's portfolio, I found myself numb and embarrassed that my intellect and intuitiveness hadn't brought this quandary to light sooner. Had I been lying to myself all along? Convincing a blind fool that everyone else had it wrong? That my time would come, and my extreme selectiveness with the world did not, in fact, keep me buried from a life of passion and prosperity, but kept me safe from the filmy tarnish society leaves unnoticed? I truly had no idea, and I certainly hadn't the time for such deconstruction. The weekend had been a wild one and I needed to unravel. Beating myself up only to find myself in the same place with the same questions was not the answer.

Melanie took a taxi home and I found myself feeling more alone than I ever had in my life. I sought solace in my work, yet it offered no reprieve, only frustration. The shapes that bullied me were in themselves a hindrance, but I would never solve them if the intolerable headaches did not cease. They were relentless, taking from me both my appetite and my sense of humor. I thought about how small their hands must be, the busy colony of lapidaries living in the confines of my head, grinding until my head shone.

The inability to paint anything discernable wasted hour after hour of supplies and my precious time. Fortunately it had been a decidedly slow time, the only things I had been working on being a nearly finished portrait of a husband and wife drawing near their fiftieth wedding anniversary—due in two months time—and a threesome of abstract pieces for a chic law firm downtown. If need be I could throw those together in a matter of days, but luckily I had nearly six weeks and the check had already been cashed. Ongoing dabbling took place for my next big show, to be held on new year's eve, which I had only been mildly excited about, the shows of the past ten years the same tasteless, beaten, misshapen dough.

Motivated for so long by the money and the recognition, I couldn't recall the last time I had actually enjoyed painting something or felt particularly proud of my work or myself the more I thought about it. Perhaps it was time I did something meaningful with my life. Perhaps it was time I relinquished the canvas, emptied the dirty water, took up rowing, or racquetball, or joined a convent. I understand the gender qualifications on the last, but I often felt boundaries needed a good pushing from time to time.

Looking at several finished works set aside for the show, I saw they all struck the same pose, all replicas or representations of something I had done before and fetched a weighted price tag for. It had all come down to what I could bring in and with how little work. I remembered telling myself in art school that it was okay if my dream was never fully lived, that the journey itself was all that I would ever need, and if more should come then it would just be the sweetest of cherries set atop. What had happened to that inspired young man who squeezed the beauty out of everything he saw and touched?

I thought perhaps a vacation was what I needed, someplace to remind me of the rest of a world that lie awake while I scornfully latched the shutters to it, perhaps to the mountains, to the plains where a drive up a steep hill could be the difference between a pair of shorts and a sweater, or maybe to an island, someplace warm where the sand massaged my toes and the sun's stronghold forced me to revel in its gaze. I closed my eyes and dreamt of a dark, yet warm place where the sky had doubled in size and the air was thick and smooth like melted chocolate. I knew not what to do, which path to trudge, which syrup to drink. Forty different bottles with healing promises abound. In the end, it mattered not where I wanted to go, for instead of the many vacations I had envisioned, I would take one of a different sort, one from the outside world, one of solitude and self-loathing.

Okay, so I'm a baby. A six-foot tall mass of water, flesh and cowardice. The reason being that the sight of blood spoon-stirs my equilibrium. I'm terribly afraid of blood and guts. Since a child, the thought of extricated innards pouring out of me was cause enough to fuel my anxiety even when faced with the most superficial of wounds. From the mere discussion of surgical processes to prime time drama emergency rooms, I could not stomach anything below the skin's surface. As I looked at the little girl sitting across from me, with the messy gauze taped to her hand I cringed and hoped my face did not overdo.

Luckily my doctor did not harbor such weakness, and sitting in his waiting room I spat my judgmental venom upon the reading material left for his supposed *valued* patients. Waiting for the sick to file in and out, sometimes out of turn (awakening jealousy and resentment from the crowd), the patients were forced to read Architectural Weekly and Golf Journal, which I could only assume added to their misery. I personally never handled the magazines, infinitely afraid of the toxic granules nestled in the flimsy pages. As a rule I attempted to make minimal contact with anything in there, and chose to supply my own book—an idea I would have thought more obvious to others—to accommodate my visit.

When I had called for an appointment, I advised the receptionist I had a sever earache, the idea coming from the story I had twisted up in the park. For years I failed to reveal my true ailments to her, as after once discovering a rash in my lower regions, embarrassed and distraught, I had told her my throat hurt. The check-in nurse made no mention of my throat, and after asking me the nature of my problem, I realized the receptionist's inquiries ended at her desk. From there on I decided my ailments were none of her business, and better discussed with those better qualified, all due respect to her filing and phone administering. Nice as pie, but helpful as two sets of lips.

One, two, three, four patients lie await ahead of me as I counted their long faces and wished to charge the office for *my* time; they had called me earlier that morning, asking me for an early arrival since they had a couple of cancellations and would be running ahead of schedule. Of course I obliged, a repeat of such an anomaly as likely as a dripless popsicle.

After waiting an hour and a half to be seen, the four and a half minute affair felt anti-climactic. Following a couple of standard neurological tests, an eye exam, and an oral questionnaire (which included: From 1 to 10, how active is your sexual life?)I was set free, the doctor's plastic smile wiped clean and renewed for the next co-pay victim.

His interpretation was that my distorted perception and nausea were due to the merciless headaches I had been having, and that the remedy to the headaches would hopefully bring swift resolve to the resulting issues. It stood to reason, and the tiny white slip I left with felt like buried treasure, and as these things happen, I felt better already.

On the way out, the receptionist told me she hoped my ears felt better, and I told her my ears were fine, it was just the voices behind them I was trying to fix.

I traced a triangle into the fog I left on the front parlor window while I searched the world outside for an answer. There were thousands of them, and sifting through the endless cotton of shapes I saw before me for the right one left me no better or worse. I watched as the happy streets ran their marathon without me, without a care or a hint of slowing. Delivery trucks and minivans cruised by my front door, packages and children being picked up and dropped off. Birds fluttered with the nerve and confidence a prom queen relishes in school the day after her crowning. I sighed, and knew I was the kid in the bathroom who had drunk too much vodka under the bleachers.

The headaches and skewed reality became more frequent, and eventually a constant, a week removed from my initial doctor's visit. I hadn't left the house the whole time, unsure of the dangers I would invite if I did. My body parts enlarged and contracted, while the walls periodically shifted, grown in some places and shrunk in others. Most of my belongings accepted their ambiguity, and functioned without protest. I, on the other hand, was not as forgiving, operating with grave difficulty, tasks such as making coffee and urinating (I was now a sitter—how embarrassing) left messes I was in no mood for. Watching television became a pointless exercise, and only listening a flirty tease. I found books amusing, a horizontal challenge. Words are truly more exciting in three dimensions, not steamrolled onto paper. I tried to bite the letters off the pages as they jumped at me, unsuccessfully, yet entertaining just the same.

After another week, and two more failed prescriptions, depression had taken its toll. I woke later and later, while the clocks taunted me, proud and stiff lipped. They hung as though their unwavering counting efforts and reluctance to quit made them better than I. Big deal. Batteries die too.

I ate only once or twice a day, and eventually the seemingly vast cupboards awaited details of the food drive that had wiped them clean. The market was the last place I was driven to go, the oppressive fluorescent bulbs striking me down, the aisles tall and indiscernible, the choices limitless, and the horror show I would endure irreversible. I had long before stockpiled enough pasta, rice, and water to last a depression. Toiletries, too, were stocked well, so my solitude came at no great cost to my lifestyle or routine. I did quickly run out of caramels, however, which was mildly tragic as I was, and forever will be, addicted to their warm, sweet taste, and I knew no place understanding and accommodating enough to deliver a box of the cubed drug to my door like a hot oven pizza. What kind of a world was it where one could not have the one rich, selfless treat of their soul's desire delivered to their stoop?

Early afternoon of a day filled with fun-house mirrors, I received a package, wrapped in paper bag brown, addressed with handwriting very familiar to me, yet I was unable to place it. No return address was listed, and upon opening it I realized I wouldn't need one. It was the children's book "The Little Engine That Could". Thank you Melanie. It was her cute, subtle (or not so) way of undercutting me and making a joke of it all at the same time. I had guessed we would be alright, so long as I kept her away from me until I got things straight. To this day, I still read the book and laugh when I am having a little self-esteem issue now and again.

In the days to come, I burnt out from the overwhelming symptoms of whatever it was that had infected me, until eventually I simply shut down, sleeping my days away, fifteen, sixteen, seventeen hours at a time, lurking in a daze the rest. Sleep became my comfortable reality, the dreams as lucid and forgiving as I could please. Once awaken, I was struck with the warped outlines of my old world, and tried to make sense of the spatial ratios, unable to match my movements to their position. My paintings had come to life and threatened my existence. My focus was pushed to its limits, bending and breaking with each step I took. Closing and opening my eyes at times revealed new versions of my house; the bed took form of a large slice of cake one second and then a pile of gelatin the next, my windows the shapes of fishbowls and fire hydrants. Moving only shifted their frowns, my bare feet with crooked toes sopping up their drool.

The phones shook a few times the first couple of days until I silenced their tears, turning them off, not caring who was caring about me. No one confronted my front door, so I was satisfied I wasn't a suspect in any murders—or thought to be dead; the disconnect of the modern world could have allowed me months as a recluse if I chose without such extreme warrants.

The drone of the outside world filled my head with silence. I lost count of the days, and after (I eventually determined) seventeen of them I stepped out of a notably long, hot shower seeing straight and feeling renewed, symptom free, a gift that brought cold chills and trepidation. I waited anxiously for the punch line, a joke I already knew and did not find amusing; strangely it did not come.

I dried quickly, then slowly, afraid of any sudden movements that might trigger a relapse. Unsure of a safe speed to travel at, the pedal on my heart thumping steadily, I dressed before I was done drying, leaving the scattered blotches of shower water on my hot skin seeping through my shirt.

Hurried, excited, clothed, and outside, I laughed at the sky, thankful for its presence and infinity. Long, deep breaths without resistance reassured me I was alive and probably would continue to be. The forms around me made their moves without worry, without despair, without knowledge that their depths were ever in question. I walked, appearing lost and bewildered, yet feeling blessed and wrapped in clean blankets, the increasing calm I enjoyed absorbing each careless step. I stayed away from liquor stores and parks, preferring the grind of the street blocks and the casual pigeons surveying their squares.

I walked for hours, thirsty for too long without quenching it. I drifted aimlessly in my promising thoughts. Was this nightmare over? A second chance was what I was being given, yes, time served in solitary confinement. I harkened back to the promises I made in my foyer, weeks back, and wondered if I would still be held to their literal verbiage. I honestly did not know if I could eat more vegetables. They simply did not agree with my taste buds.

It was a pleasant day, the thin cloud cover only a dimmer setting the tranquil mood, and I saw that the day's shape and pulse differed not than any other. Hours would pass and the light would eventually die out, giving way to an endless blackness where secrets and broken promises hide. The days were all the same in that structural regard, yet the trivial doings scattered within them were different, changing only the shapes and expressions of the faces that patrolled its sidewalks. I breathed deep, intoxicating breaths of oxygen and relief as often as I could and continued to thank whatever had made it possible for me to return to the normalcy of my silly world.

Miles from home I noticed a stone wall accompanying my walk shoulder high to the left, clean grass stretching up it, heavily spotted with short and tall chiseled stones, and I realized where I was, my wandering and smiling having blinded my sense of direction. The graveyard was well-groomed and the peculiar look of disdain it held stood as a warning of things to come.

I quickly turned my head to catch sight of a slight, white rabbit scurrying across the grass, who then stopped and stared at me, its fur coat dulled in the sun's absence. The innocent creature, as if unimpressed, took quick note of my poor existence, and bounced off, up the hill.

"Wait up, Peter," I said, and kept moving, curious where he was headed.

The entrance to the dearly departed museum greeted me with a sturdy frown when I turned the corner to the paved path, and with a tap on my own shoulder I remembered who lie there. I wished it had all been a hoax, the greatest of mind tricks pulled on me, and in the end poof it never actually happened. I hadn't been to my parents' grave in years, at first making it an annual visit—in time making it an afterthought. I told myself the visits I paid them in my head, in my dreams, in my memories, were sufficient, and that if asked, they would agree that I needn't kneel on their grassy roof to prove my love. I continued to walk up the hill, embarrassed and worried I was in trouble.

Movement up ahead shook me from my daze, and again the unassuming rabbit, clad in nothing but ivory—I thought to remind it Labor Day had now passed—toyed with my focus. It waited, as if playing usher for the occasion, then took off up the hill hoping I would give chase.

I entered casually and glanced at the upright, rigid stones, hands in my pockets, assuming the role of victim.

I did not particularly enjoy cemeteries, and knew no one who did, yet in this particular one I always got a laugh when passing the grave of Antoine Seagall, a long time golf pro in our city. Around his tombstone, the bean shaped floor was carpeted with Creeping Bent Grass, mowed fine to a putting green, dotted with a real hole to putt into.

Beneath a dark, brittle, outstretched tree sat my parents' grave. I turned my head, as though distracted, when the names appeared, and suddenly I was struck with the sight and shock of the earth sinking in before me, the graves ahead all trapped in the new folds of the grassy earth pressed together. I stopped and watched as the carpet of waves went on up and over the hill, the top barely in sight, marked by a statue of a little girl (whose bronzed head I could now only see) who refused to leave our town in the late seventeenth century because she was fond of all the blueberries that grew on her family's land, so the tale is told. The girl's father had wanted nothing more in the world than to make his daughter happy beyond her imagination, so he decided to stay when all of the other settlers thought the land cursed because of a fatal sickness that swept through the surrounding communities, killing hundreds. He declared himself the owner of the land after all others had departed, and fortunately, in time, more settlers came to the place I would eventually call home.

I tried to move closer but the cold, dry ground sunk into a pit of nothing in every direction around their grave to within inches of my worn out sneakers, no longer gleaming white in their newness, but faded around the edges like an old, worn paperback. The tree that loomed above giving marginal shade cover from the east stood tall, it's thick, earthed roots now an abyss of black space, deep and uninviting. I looked down into the cavernous opening and fear swallowed me. The dead, innocent faces of hundreds of trapped souls, none I could identify, funneled down into a secret darkness I was in no hurry to meet. Although none of the illusions I had seen to this point had been true, I took this to be a sign which demanded compliance. I jumped back, looking away, pretending I had not just seen what I knew I had. Frightened, spooked, alarmed, I turned about face and sulked out of the cemetery as fast as possible, clutching my arms to my chest, a huddled figure expelled from the shadows and onto the black and white streets, relieved and heavy hearted.

That same night I slept ten hours, woke to a dried mouth, and drank the slow hum of my ceiling fan. What oh what would this day bring? I was sure to find out and wasted no time getting started. Up with ease and anticipation I quickly found I detested the walls, the corners, the lines, the floors, and the pressure they collectively forced upon me. Without eating, I washed my face and dressed to run, my heart needing to pump, the sky in need of a greater audience.

Outside the door my skin welcomed the atmospheric change in the excited form of thousands of tiny bumps on my skin risen like fresh bread. I decided to head first to the graveyard and make up for my quick exit the night before. Hopefully my folks had forgiven me, and understood the obstacles which I had to overcome were not of my own doing. I felt guilty—although yesterday's pit of death was not of my doing—and decided to bring my mother flowers; dad couldn't care less. I did not want to bring a bouquet of guilt, as a man does to his wife after staying out too late with the fellas the night before; I wished to bring flowers of appreciation and adoration. If she could read my thoughts still, as she had been so adept at doing, she would see my struggle, my plight, my regret, and accept the heartfelt gesture.

I stopped halfway into a florist overflowing with greenery and homemade signs that read "peace" and "laugh" and "fresh flowers sold here". The cute, polite old woman inside, dutifully cropping the ends off of roses, brightened as I stepped forth. I had never known a disgruntled florist, and wondered if all the oxygen spouting about had a hand in that.

"Hello, young man." Keep going. "How may I help you?"

"I am looking for some flowers." No kidding.

"Well lucky for you I have one or two lying around here someplace!" Her warm disposition reminded me of the woman in the park who had helped nurse me back to my senses. I wished it had been her helping me now, and wondered if I would ever see her again.

"Daisies."

I wandered around the room and admired all of the smells and colors that surrounded me. I could see myself arranging flowers all day long, making cute little bouquets of daffodils and whatever went with daffodils.

"You're all set," the old woman informed me, and I reached for my cash.

"What's the damage?"

"Well, let's see," she said looking up at the invisible adding machine above her head, "Four times seven is fourteen, so fourteen!" Her math had me puzzled, but it was nothing new these days, so I let it go, the way of so many other recent things, and paid up.

Flowers were not my expertise by any means, but I knew mom's favorites to be daisies. I remembered dad buying them on occasion, and the first time I had seen them I asked him what they were, not knowing there were different varieties, thinking daisies were all yellow with dark centers. I had confused them with sunflowers, as daisies come in a pleasant variety of hues and sizes. She fancied the purple breed, with yellow centers, and in a rush of good fortune I was able to arrive at their grave with exactly those, along with my heart where my sleeve would normally have been had I not been running in a tank top. I reconsidered my clothes when I reached the hill of the dead, hoping no one, including my parents, would think my attire disrespectful. The justification I served argued that it mattered not what pieces of stitched cotton hung from my body any more than why the pudding's rat race was never on ice, as such trivial things were even more so where I was headed.

My sight was functioning properly and I was thankful for the reprieve. Up the hill towards their resting place, I felt confident, daisies in hand, and I recited the lines in my head I would read to them. I would apologize for not coming sooner, for being selfish as usual, for allowing my own problems to come before them—for being me. I would explain what had been happening, the frustration it had brought, and the self imprisonment I had endured to wash away its grime. *It's okay,* they would say, but *excuses* they would think, and I would assure them I would make no more of those, for they had gotten me nowhere except lost, a place I had grown tired of.

Twenty yards from their lawn I saw my old friend again. Peter peered at me and it looked as though a trap were set and he were the bait.

I'm not chasing you, mister rabbit. No time for games, today, sorry.

He ran off over the hill and I couldn't resist, taking off after him but clumsily stumbled on the crushed gravel and sand of the tight, winding path which led in my parents' direction, then jutted left and weaved around the backside of the hill to where my friend was now hiding. I fell to the ground, palms out, daisies cast aside. The coarse rug marred my palms, and tiny pricks of blood rose to the surface. Looking up I saw nothing but tall waves of grass, their peaks over ten feet in height, and my destination grave obstructed by their stance. Again, doubt waded through my veins, yet I tried to move forward, walking into another grave but seeing nothing but green, the stone obstacle nowhere to be found. I turned around and found normalcy in my wake, yet back around again the forms the graveyard had taken on resembled nothing I could discern. This encore presentation was less amusing than its premier and I left wanting my money back.

6

The ebb of routine came without protest on my part. I only wanted to feel normal again and get back to living my predictable life without turning a corner and getting punched in the face, and for a few days I did. I busied myself so not to overthink or lie in dirty, shallow graves of pity. I spent my time chasing angles, banging knees off coffee tables, and seducing anyone who might be entertaining the idea of hanging something artsy on their wall.

I sought to take advantage of every opportunity which presented itself, not knowing if an untimely end was near, or how it would come. Increasing the number linked to the success of my savings account had always been a reassuring accomplishment. The lunches I bought and the tireless rhetoric I shared with the uppity, crass, and the uneducated were the price I paid for my good fortune's comfortable chair. It was not until I looked into the mirror on a wealthy couple's living room wall one evening and was embarrassed by what I saw, that I realized just how phony I could be at times and how manufactured the conversation I worked within was too. And as I was good at doing, I paid the thought no more attention and allowed it to fuel my greed.

Selling yourself is an easy task when you too would actually buy in, and that was the attitude I projected. The attention my name drew was not what I had anticipated, after two people in direct contact with me, and another by my front door, had met untimely deaths, yet the buzz surrounding my name drove up interest, creating a backlog of work I would need a clone to complete.

Unfortunately I could not even start. The emptiness of creative thought which presided as I sought to cash in on my opportunities was a first. For days I did nothing but eye the slabs of white that taunted me, hoping that that which had infiltrated my body and mind would succumb to my fortitude. I could not force the issue, and it would not come with encouragement, much like sleep. I tried painting with music, without, with the grownup grape juice and without, night and day, left handed and right; the pool was dry, and desperation hovered with the smell of wet towels in a latched hamper.

I did, however, manage to complete the portrait which needed finishing, an easy task, much like paint by numbers. Two weeks were still left for me to complete the law firm pieces, yet without a little motivation, I would find myself issuing a refund check for five thousand dollars. Nothing else I tried proved encouraging, the purulent gravy of paint I splashed amounting to nothing. Oh the crimes!

I looked for answers, as I so often did, with a jog in the park. The trees were dressed in new suits, standing tall, welcoming my visit to their sanctuary, ambassadors of serenity, their yellow-greens hugging the amber leaves just in. A ripe, out of the dryer freshness owned the air, and it nibbled the inside of my nose, a soft blanket tossed over my shoulders, and I inhaled all of it that I could, cleansing my soul and the demons that sought to further corrupt it.

My legs had lost a bit of their resolve due to the recent inactivity, but the burn they conjured up reminded me they still knew of their commitments. My thighs ached, yet the lactic acid gurgling inside was not enough to stunt my efforts. I studied everything and everyone, trying to peel off an enlightenment with which to transfer to my work. I measured the contrasting dynamics between the old and the young, and decided I would never grow old. The maturity and sense of belonging supposedly inherited with age were something of an illusion, I felt, something to hang their wigs on, so those unmindful of the passing days would not frown upon their deterioration with pity, nor skip them in the head count.

I passed by the quaint playground, housed in black fencing and floored with padded cement, and watched it swirl with a group of after-school hostages. To be young in the twenty first century is not what it used to be, as the age old adage proclaims. It never is though, and the youth will always roll their eyes when hearing it told. I watched these six to ten year olds, a pair with hand held video games, another with headphones, one talking on a cell phone, and the others enjoying their six minutes on the jungle gym until their short attentions forced a quick transition to the next station. These kids didn't have it made, they had it made *for* them. With no sense of sacrifice, appreciation of anything noble, or the ability to make decisions for themselves, how could they be expected to cope in a world with endless options? What kind of a life is it where everything and anything is possible yet never knowing or believing for more than a minute?

I decided to stop by the chess tables and thank the elders for their assistance one more time. Cries of a vociferous nature would not greet my strategic statesmen (and women) this time around as I sauntered towards the herd gathered about as they always were. The aura of the group felt the same when I arrived, much like the awkwardness of wearing another's undergarments. Looking at this pack of moving statues, I felt insignificant, lost...then I saw her face. Oh that smile!

"Hello, blue eyes." she said, hands on her hips. Her name was Claire, and with an air dried composure I noticed how striking her beauty was, even at an advanced age. The fringe of her eyes told me she had seen more than sixty of these triumphant summers hand the baton over to autumn. Regardless, her small frame revealed she had taken care of herself, and I felt like a boy attracted to his mother's friend. I eye painted her body. At least I could paint *something.*

"Hello you..." I said, grinning.

"How are the ears?" she asked, her voice as pleasant as could be.

"Huh?" Confused at first, I wondered what my ears had to do with anything, then in a camera flash I recalled the fib I had told. "Oh yeah, the noise." I shook my head, "No, no repeat of that."

"Glad to hear."

"Thank you again...you were sweet."

"Aww, shucks." She shuffled her feet deliberately.

Something about this woman made me want to unclothe her, and something else made me want to run. The thought of toying with Mel's heart popped into my head and I wondered if I should leave the pretty old woman be. My energy and excitement faded in these thoughts, so with a stiff, cold knob I shut them off. I looked past her shoulder to the rest of the group and decided I had nothing in common with them and had no desire to hang around much longer.

"So do you play?" I asked, pointing a finger toward the group.

She scrunched her soft skin and made a silly face that tickled me within. "A little bit, but it's more of a social exercise out here, more checkers going on than chess...if you catch my drift."

Her smile revealed gleaming whites, and I wrestled the

strange ideas fighting for air time in my head. Just then, one from the drool pool looked at me from under his fedora and the face grabbed my core, giving it a shake. I could not place the man, but he looked vaguely familiar, the disapproving face warning me to watch my step. I briefly lost what Claire was saying, and apologized.

"I'm sorry, what was that?"

"What's wrong?" she asked, trying to read my expression.

"Oh nothing, sorry, thought I recognized someone. What was that you asked?"

"Oh, I just asked if *you* played."

"Not in years," I said and counted them in her wrinkles, wondering what they tasted like. "So how often do you come down here? Are you retired?" I hoped my question did not insinuate she looked old, and pried my foot from the back of my mouth.

She laughed, putting her hand over her mouth and turning towards the group. I searched for openings in her fingers, specks of ivory teasing my view.

"No, not retired *just* yet. I work in a rehab center, the Horizon, and I pop in here after some afternoons to see a couple of my favorites. Jimmy there with the hat (she nodded to the man whose look moments before had burned a hole in me, the smoke still lingering), he's got a bit of a crush on me, and Gertie down at the end there holding the coffee, laughing her head off, she's one of my girls. I had Charlie in there for a spell too, you met him and his porridge, but he's a bit out to lunch. Sweet as pie though!"

While she pointed out her friends I quickly took note and then shifted to her profile, the skin wrapped tightly over her skull hinting at her age, and I found it most appealing. We exchanged comfortable small talk and I wanted to confess what had been happening to me, the folds around her eyes telling of a compassion and understanding I might be wise to confide in.

There was clearly an unspoken energy between us, and I thought we both were fighting it's existence, unsure which pawn to put forth. I didn't realize what I was doing until the words were already out. "Hey, would you like to grab lunch sometime, just the two of us?"

She playfully put a pink-nailed finger to her open lip and looked to the sky as if something divine were giving her permission. Again the smile I had hoped see came to the surface. "You sure you want to be seen in public with an old hag like me?"

"You kidding?" I asked, quietly second-guessing my actions. "You sure you want to be seen with a little boy like me?" Say no. You can do it. I agree, this is silly.

"How about tomorrow?"

Tomorrow came. We failed to discuss the evident twenty year or so age gap separating us, instead talking generalities on love, life, books, movies, and of course, art. Claire was still active, and knew the value of a smart diet, which explained the healthy glow her skin gave off. She even ice skated twice a week down at the town arena and took in a step class when she had the time. I pictured myself on skates and shuddered.

She was charming and quite confident in her convictions. She spoke of the future, as if her life were in its infancy, speaking of someday finding love and having a family, and eventually traveling the world.

"When you think of it, most people spend their entire lives within a twenty mile radius," she said, looking out into the park where we had met, "knowing only the landscape which can barely be seen on the tip of a pin on a map as big as a house."

"Is that such a bad thing?"

"Happy people will say no, but even so I think there is so much more they are missing out on. Just because you are born someplace doesn't mean you are destined to die there."

"True, so I'm guessing you like to travel?"

"Like it? No, I absolutely love it, the different streets and buildings and peoples and the skies. Oh my how the sky looks so different in new places!"

I had traveled a fair amount, but listening to Claire speak of it I wondered if I had missed out on it altogether. She continued and the words drowned in my thoughts of meeting her twenty or thirty years younger, and how I would have liked to have traveled with her.

I had chosen a small café nearby to meet, for I loved that

part of the city and the picture that it held, a steady pulse of leisure and obligation found in the movements of those around. A busy street with two lanes in each direction separated us from the outer rim of the park. The rush of the cars brushed up against the calm of green grass, each dangerously close to giving in to its neighbor. The water could be seen through the trees, and the reflection of the sun peeked through offering the tease of a future filled with wonder.

I often pretended that I were one of the pedestrians I saw and tried to envision what was going through their heads. A stiff man with a dark suit and aviator glasses walked past and I thought he must think his socks did not smell. I quickly honed in on another, half my age, carrying a backpack in his right hand, dressed for a day of lounging in his boarder shorts and open-toed sandals. I pictured the bag to be filled with snacks and books, and imagined him to be content in not having any worries from which to be burdened, and thought it might be nice to feel the wind, or an ant or two, on my toes.

Claire had a charming twinkle in her eyes when she spoke, which told that life had not calcified her spirit. I envied it, feeling at forty two the world had shown me enough ugly expressions to support facelifts. Claire did not need one, physically or metaphorically. Her lips, which had lost the perk and fullness I imagined them to have had many years ago, tempted me, and I decided that if at some point she wanted me to, I would kiss them, not thinking of the consequences or the emotions and hopes built by pursuing such curiosities. After all, what expectations could she have possibly held? Informed of my hopes to fall in love someday and have children, she echoed the sentiment, perhaps an inference to adoption or some awkward surrogate mother situation. I knew not, but I had to weigh whether it was wise to further anything with this woman who made me feel home as a grandmother might, except with lips I wanted to seize.

An hour passed in what seemed like a minute, my cheeks sore from over-smiling. Not the necessary charade you enact when someone bores you and you smile at everything they say to be polite, yet have nothing to offer in return so you keep on smiling, and listening, but smiling which makes you forget you had ever done so before.

I paid the check after holding up a hand to protest her adding a share, and while I sat digesting she caught me daydreaming again, a skill I had perfected, silencing all that sought to permeate its walls. I was busy arguing with myself when she cut in.

"Vey," She took me by the hand, hers fragile with raised veins I could see. "It's okay, you can just say no, I won't be crushed or anything. I know we're a few years apart, but just for fun, if nothing else."

"No, yeah...sure!" I said, not exactly sure of what I had agreed to.

"Okay, so a movie it is. Hope you like horror flicks."

"Yes, of course." I had been living one recently, what was one more?

"I wasn't sure if this was a good idea when you asked me to lunch, but I like you, and I think I can trust you, so as long as you don't kidnap me and chop me up into pieces..."

I laughed aloud and convinced myself there was no harm in a movie, that doing so I was bound to no contract forgoing my desires of longevity and hope, no proclamation of love and eternity, and that I hadn't been to the cinema in a while, so I was overdue; worst case, I ended up with a new friend. She was cute, endearing—inspiring even—,made me laugh, and I adored how she made light of our age difference. Try new things I told myself, make new friends, or *old* ones.

"Okay, deal!" I said. "I'll have my parents sign a permission slip and you make sure to take your calcium pills."

Cue punch in the face: On my walk home a couple of cars shot past me in the same feverish fashion they had my first night (I refer to it as my first night, a coining reserved for new year's, but my first night was the start of a new life, and not just a new calendar, so I felt I had rights to borrow its use). Claire and I had parted ways at the café, leaving me alone in a virtual maze. She had to get back to work and I had to get back to feeling bad for myself. I scolded myself for thinking I was better. Why was this happening? Did I really deserve this?

I tried not to panic, hoping it was just a glitch in the system. It wasn't. The streets had widened, the double lanes stretched out a hundred feet and the sky became dark with mudded water, calm ripples making their way across it. Again, the sounds were what they should have been, but failed to match the moving pictures behind them. I slammed my eyes shut, unable to slow my pulse, which shot up along side my increasing worry.

"No. Please, no..." I said softly, trying to wish the evil away, breathing in through my nose and out my mouth.

Opening my eyes, I was relieved to see the freshly narrow streets busy with traffic and sausages again. The sky, however, still threatened to wash me away with its current. I raised my walk to a jog and kept my head down, peeking up occasionally to heed the wild currents overhead, yet I remained shaken and dry. The heavy black shoes I wore were not suited for running, but I did my best. After only a block my feet hurt, and I was forced to walk again. Breathing heavily, I realized I was on the very block where my late friend in gray had asked me what I knew of time. I knew that too much had passed recently without my approval. This had to end, I demanded to fate. I simply would not wash out with the black tide above.

Was this someone or something trying to tell me something dear and dire? Had my streak of good luck and fortune run its course? Had my cup runneth over? I feared a repeat of the horror I experienced before, and fortunately no one died during this walk, although I felt death's shadow consistently dancing across my path with the cold chills it sent up my shirt.

At home the disparities continued, the weeks spent bonding with them making the adjustment easier, and though the depths and size of things continually changed, I was beginning to decipher their masks more quickly. The headaches came and went with the days, and their stabbing at times sunk me to my knees. What horrible pain! I could think of no one who deserved such evil, so why oh why was I the proprietor of such a madhouse?

The next day I went in for more tests. An MRI and CT Scan revealed nothing. Caring less about my sight and more about the ground shattering skull attacks, I tried my fifth prescription. Within a half hour of ingestion the headaches and nausea had completely ceased, although my studio appeared inside out—a minor detail a quick tumble dry would hopefully wring out.

"Yahtzee!" I cried out. Small wonders.

I tried to paint, fresh with new ideas for the first time in a long time, but the mess I made compared to a preschooler's sloppy water color. I had difficulty touching the brush to a canvas that would not stop moving, or scarcely resembled a canvas, and when I did, the displaced strokes I left were explosions, a war of paint I had apparently jumpstarted. Hours passed with little result; a blindfolded effort might have rendered more success—an idea I had not thought of at the time.

The debate raged on in my head, whether to cancel my

show or produce a new series of rubbish and pass it off as something it wasn't. Did it matter? I had enough money saved and invested to last me a year in hiatus—or two even; I could wait it out, fritter away my savings and my days, and return from the grave reborn. Perhaps that was what I needed, a rebirth, a resurrection, one which would force the opening of wallets and collect what a year of reflection and soul searching could produce. I decided that if by Halloween I had not gotten a fix on my work, I would do just that.

At the close of another day which could have been a Monday or Friday or not, as they all held the same insignificance, the sanitary glare of my bathroom severed the darkness and kicked awake my consciousness. I hoped the length of the recent days would not be a constant theme. Brushing my teeth, I looked into the mirror and asked the confused face peering back: "What am I doing?" which came out a foamy spattering of sounds. "What the hell is wrong with me?" More spatter. The face looking back was altered, pale, sad. It did not answer and I stared at it as the white and watered paste trickled down my chin. I couldn't figure how someone as tanned as I knew I should look to appear so remorse and pallid under the light. The mirror was guilty of misrepresentation, so I spit, wiped, hit the switch, then remembered to pee—in the dark, certain I had miscalculated a wee bit—and went to sleep. No, not in the bathroom.

7

Making love to a woman in her sixties, in the dark, is very much akin to making love to a woman forty years her junior. I found this out not long after taking Claire to the movies where she forced my hand, quite literally, taking it from me and caressing it gently through the second half of the predictable junk spread thick on the screen before us.

Her hand was soft and warm, yet after envisioning the blue-gray veins that I knew highlighted them, I wished that I never had agreed to the date in the first place. Then when she rubbed my leg in the fashion she did, I wished she would slide her hand down my pants.

Needless to say I was conflicted. On the one hand, she was old. On the other, we clicked. Her charm, energy, and wit had been a life preserver for my sinking soul, and I easily forgot my woes when in her company. She wielded such optimistic impressions of the day at hand and the future, however long or short hers might be. It had me rethinking everything I knew.

For what *did* I know? Not a great deal, I concluded. I

knew how to take a gift, a skill, and turn it into profit. I knew how to manipulate people and direct them towards my needs, I knew to smile when I needed to, or to saddle up on the back of injustice when it made me appear better than those looking up at the judgmental line of morality. I knew in a world full of untruths, the only honesty I could count on was the dialogue in my head, and that however light or dark its shade compared to the paint that covered the earth with mediocrity, I would never trust those spoken from another without trying them before the jury seated within.

True, my instincts had not always served me right, but who knew better than I how to live my life? Who truly knew me better than I? No one. In fact, no one really knew me at all, so what blueprint was I to follow that wasn't designed specifically for me? Why build a house using the plans for another lot? Why, as an army, go to war with the playbook from a high school football team? Why carry out my days based on someone else's ideas, based solely on their personal successes and failures and interpretations of reality?

As much as I believed myself to be an independent nation, free from oppression, I was still all too influenced by outside sources, from the media and public perception, to the clothes I wore and the cars I drove; I dressed to impress, and spoke to evoke.

I deemed the movies a safe place to take Claire, her jest that I might not want to be seen in public with her still fresh in my mind. I calculated the actual time people might see us to be very minimal, perhaps five to ten minutes between buying tickets, snacks, and finding seats—even less after, the walk to the car our only exposure. A couple hours in a dark theater, no one could make me out, or whom I was with—no judgments to be made, no gossip to stir up, no lumps to knead out with hands I wasn't sure I could count on any longer.

The fright show we watched did little to provoke fears of any sort from revealing their faces within mine, although Claire did suffer a couple of momentary setbacks, marked by her clinging to my arm and leg while turning her head to avoid the unfolding bludgeoning on the screen. Time seemed to be in a rush to be somewhere, and we were back in the warmth of my house in what seemed like seconds since Claire had picked me up.

We procured fire that night, another bottle of wine uncorked by my hand, another precarious situation I opened the door to. Her body was slender and firm, and she had lost a great deal of the muscle I assumed her to have had, but it made no difference. My dimly lit bedroom did wonders for the unfolding scene, and my finicky taste had taken exception to this woman who smelled of pressed roses and melting snow.

After many renewed breaths and echoes of pleasure I lay entangled with her, pleasantly surprised by the warmth we produced, delighted with the uninhibited nature she displayed, and impressed with the experience she showed between the sheets.

Beside her I laughed, expressing my satisfaction. “I tell you, when I fell that day, this is the last place I expected we would be.”

“Oh c’mon, you can’t tell me you weren’t thinking it when you first saw me. I saw you checking me out!”

I dared not tell her that I inspect everyone, and that she had been no different, because it wasn’t entirely true. The part about checking everyone out was, but I will admit her particular lines had me curious, yet of her earlier playing days.

“Okay, you got me, but you’re lucky I didn’t run off with your friend there, with the fur wall around her neck. I knew I was taking one of you home with me.”

We laughed out loud, picturing the obvious retiree whose thickly oppressive summer scarf made one wonder just how cold a neck could truly be to deserve such decorative protection.

“Well I checked you out too, lying there like a drunken bum...a cute drunken bum though.”

“Well thank you...everyone needs loving.” Especially me, I thought.

“You think so?”

“I do, it’s what makes this crazy world spin.”

“And without it?”

“Without it people trudge through in a daze, unsure of their next move, afraid, apprehensive, fearing the wrong steps.” Was I talking about myself?

“I think people comprehend their own mortality more than you realize.”

"I don't know if it's a question of mortality, do you?"

"I do, actually. You are blessed with "x" number of days here, in this world, correct?"

"Uh-huh." I replied, nodding.

"So I will grant you that most hope to find love, and many, too, are miserable without it, but only because of their impending death. If you were to tell the same people they would live to be a thousand without fail, would the urgency be as severe? Would love be as necessary and pressing if there were literally forever to find it in its purest, most intoxicating form?"

"Well now you're talking about time—"

"Yes, because everything has a relativity to time. In this case, the desire for your heart's end-all gratification in the form of an emotional union."

"Okay then how do you explain a twenty year old ready to kill himself because his girlfriend left him and he thinks his life is over? He still has a good sixty to eighty years left to find love, so why the meltdown? Because all he wants is love."

"You're talking about the aftermath of a seemingly traumatic emotional situation. Talk to the same kid in two years, or even one. If he's still upset and alone, and still in a hurry to find the so-called love of his life, tell me his motivations aren't then somehow linked to his ultimate fear of death. Maybe fear isn't the word, but receptiveness to its inevitability."

"I suppose, but there are plenty of people that same age

who are depressed and feel hopeless and lost because merely because they haven't found someone, and they know, and are often told, that they have an entire lifetime."

"Again, back to death. A hundred years is not a long time, and certainly not a given—eighty even shorter—and then there is the uncertainty of disease or a fatal accident which any of us are susceptible to. It makes time feel a great deal shorter than it's probable course. The young who you speak of see people of all ages unhappily alone and fear that same fate comes from missed opportunity within a sliver of time. Plus they're kids, undeveloped emotionally and in the right side of their brains. Damn dopamine!"

I busied my fingers on her skin. "Alright, but you have to stipulate that the end all desire is love. And perhaps time is what makes its legend so prevalent, but you speak of a hypothetical and I'm all about the here and now." I could not keep my hands off her even during serious matters.

"You speak in such absolutes, too, as if love is the end all for everyone!"

"Well maybe I'm all about absolutes, too. I absolutely love touching you..."

"Apparently, mister busy hands."

I busied them some more. "All I know is everyone deserves some loving at some point, if only for a little while."

"Even an old gal like me?" She hid under the sheets, awaiting my chase.

"Even a young swan like you..." I said, and dove in.

She stayed the night after a small dose of encouragement on my part. For the first time in a long time I had felt at ease, detached from the clocks and the chatter of the outside world. She wielded this calming influence gracefully, and opposing the demands my sleeping habits made, I welcomed her occupation and sunk into the comfort of her presence. I was accustomed to sleeping alone, but at the same time I had been accustomed to sleeping with women my own age. What was the difference really? If it made me equally happy to mold body pretzels with this woman compared to one half her age, what difference did it make? I told myself that she would die well before my time, and that was the difference. She was right, it was all about mortality.

I discovered why I did not date women who attended high school in the nineteen sixties upon awakening the next morning. At a quarter past seven, the streets warming with the sun's building breath, I was rattled by a frying pan clacking the stovetop, a sound I knew not of the dreamy world I was grinning in. I heard a soft, flowery voice singing happily to itself. When I first noticed the time, my head had been heavy and immobile, my eyelids a matching pair of castle doors. Activity before the stroke of ten was early for me, so this had been offensive. My first thoughts were that I had gone and screwed up again. I had allowed my wandering eye to lead me down a thorny path filled with vague twists and turns, leaving doubt of my proximity to the actual intended trail.

Up with a stagger and several groans of habit, I lumbered to the kitchen, enticed by smells of morning treats, which turned out to be fresh batter and melted butter. I caught sight of her slight figure, hair up and cute as a pony, and this piqued my interest. I hoped the taste would equal even a fraction of the pleasure it seemed to promise. Of the pancakes.

She whirled around, sensing my appearance.

"Morning...*morning* turtle..."

"*Morning* turtle?" I rubbed the back of my gray, buzzed head and joined her by the stove.

"Yes, morning turtle, it's an ordinary turtle, just slower 'cause it's morning."

"Cute," I said smiling, not nearly awake enough to appreciate, nor delight, in such silliness.

"Yeah, I can be," she said and continued to float like an angel with new wings.

I generally possessed a healthy appetite after waking, yet this day I was mindful of a stomach that wrestled with guilt, pleasure, and doubt.

"What's going on here? You didn't have to do this, Claire."

"I know, but it was the only way I could get some free food out of this, and show off a little talent of mine at the same time." She walked by me with plates in hand and I followed, planting myself on a counter stool I paid far too much for. Goodness, it was only a stool.

Relieved there was no good morning kiss, I studied her moves. The innocent grin she wore never seemed to flicker and it spawned one of my own. I watched her thin, freckled legs that fell out of the large tee shirt she had snatched from my closet. Mildly annoyed by this breach, I decided the theft was forgivable, since she had made me breakfast.

"How did you sleep?" she asked, and slipped a pair of modest pancakes onto my plate, turning to fetch the mangled eggs. I could see letters being scrambled, but eggs were clearly mangled.

"Great, I think. I think I'm still doing it...sleeping."

"Well, you can go back after you fill up...I can't stay long, work is waiting, but I thought I would start your day off right, after you ended my night with this smile I can't seem to get rid of."

After a small sampling of her own pancakes and eggs, delicious by all measurable accounts, Claire jumped up and ran into the bedroom, changed quickly, then hopped back into the kitchen still buttoning her jeans. She apologized for the quick exit (which I loved), gave me a soft, moist, good-bye kiss, and wished me a wonderful day. The glow she left was purple and pink with white highlights dancing on top.

A few bites later, my mouth pleased, I stumbled back off the stool when the second pancake on my plate turned into a dozen mini pancakes, symmetrically placed in a square. This didn't send me far, but the glass of milk Claire had poured, which sat twenty feet high, did. I fell to the floor, fork still in hand, my cheeks filled with food. I resumed chewing and got up, reclaimed my position on the stool and saw the counter had nearly filled up my spacious kitchen, stretching forty feet in every direction. Quite the feast could be had on this ridiculous sight, and I decided Thanksgiving dinner would be moved from the dining room to the kitchen counter. If only I had someone to invite.

The jackhammer in my head then came to life, protesting its sedentary lifestyle, sending me crawling for manufactured relief. The miracle drug whose name I cannot spell or pronounce once again managed to subdue the pain, yet left my sight drunken and unresponsive to reason.

Other than the issues with my vision, I felt fine. Restless, I knew I wouldn't sleep another wink, and decided to paint. It was early, but I was up, fueled, and motivated. I headed to the basement as if I owned it. Well I did, so it wasn't an act. I headed to the basement as if I were about to teach it a lesson, show it how things worked around here. Sadly, frustration played badminton with me and I lost, an imaginary broken racket and real tears all that remained. I wasted hour after hour trying to put down what I saw in my mind's eye, but the colors, shapes, and sizes I created did not match. How much money in wasted canvas had I lost? How much more of this torture would I have to endure, and why was I the victim, what lesson was I supposed to learn?

By dinner I was finally seeing straight, but terribly exhausted. All the motivation stored in me had been sapped and I truly believed it was over. The calendar said there was still time, but I wasn't buying it. I had three weeks until Halloween, the self imposed deadline to get my act together or take up fishing. Perhaps not fishing, as sitting for hours at a time not actually doing anything was not the most exciting thing I could think of. I would become a sculptor, or a poet, or a collector of model trains. Exciting, I know!

When I made the obligatory call to Claire that night, I had intended to end it, her mortality theory helping to solidify my reasoning, but somehow managed to invite her over again the next night. I wanted to avoid the public eye for the night while I continued to contemplate my level of involvement. She made no suggestions, agreeing to a quiet night in and I gave her silent praise for the lack of maintenance she required.

I showered and wasted the night in front of the television, falling asleep there, the crease of the couch splitting my cheek, sure to leave an imprint for hours after I woke.

The next day was uneventful as I slept until two and moped until six. Claire called in the middle someplace to confirm her arrival at seven, and before she did, I showered and ate, feeling rested and looking forward to her company.

Her clothes spoke of someone unable to accept the truth of her age. The tight jeans and tiny pink tank she wore were by no means unattractive, but the effort to narrow our gap was a bit obvious and unnecessary. While I believed her to be in her early sixties, her energy made me feel I was fifteen all over again. She didn't need to dress it. She looked healthier and happier than anyone I knew, at any age.

Her lips melted beneath mine when we kissed, then hardened and melted again with each gasp while we curled up and watched a movie on the couch. My stomach possessed the same fuzzy resonance it had thirty years before, afraid my mother would catch me making out with Shelly Michaud, my first certified girlfriend. Under the agreement that there be no "funny business," as my mother put it, we were allowed to watch television and play board games in our family's finished basement. The spiral iron steps that lead upstairs gave us more than enough time to relocate to opposite ends of the couch should someone decide to descend, thanks to the cramped design. If you weighed in over two hundred pounds your best bet was to take the cellar door from the outside.

The anticipation of the naughty things to come excited me and worried me just the same. The previous night I had embraced Claire's imperfections, but I wondered if I would fall into old habits and be repulsed by them. Since women a fraction of her age had soured my stomach, what would stop the same from happening with her? Melded with her on the couch, I looked down at the patch of freckles decorating her chest and neck, then decided to worry another day.

Fortunately, I had seen the movie we were watching, otherwise my wandering mind would have ruined the picture. I counted down the minutes to make my move, but before the moment came that I had deemed an appropriate time to attack, she struck first.

Whatever multivitamin she had been taking, I decided I would too, immediately, and after three hours of rhythmic gymnastics on top of my bed we let our hearts beat at a more relaxed pace. She nestled her head into my chest and read the brail of my body with her free hand.

"My, If you've lost a step with age, I'd have had a hard time keeping up with you before then."

"Me? What about you? You're like Wonder Woman."

She playfully bit my arm. "Oh yeah, by the way, I parked my ship in the back yard, hope you don't mind. It's invisible." She rolled over to steal a sip of water from the nightstand, revealing a painful looking burn at the base of her back.

"Oh in that case, no worries." I traced her spine with my hand, down to its end, gently over the burn.

"Oh, that. Drunken mistake. Long time ago. Feels funny huh?"

I said nothing, choosing to become one with her body, pressing my front into her back, inhaling her petals.

She dared to confront the impatient zebra in the corner of the room. An elephant would not have fit. "So what do you think people will say about us?"

"That we smile too much."

"No, seriously, do you even care how old I am, because you haven't asked once."

"No, not really." Liar. "Well, yes...but I'm trying not to...maybe it doesn't matter." She turned and stared at me, waiting for more, and I obliged. "I think it matters if we are trying to set expectations, and if so what those are should be addressed, but I feel that here and now, we are good, and it does not make a difference just yet. I like the mystery." I realized my choice of words made her seem like a science experiment or that I didn't take her or the possibility of us seriously. I decided to reel her back in and talk my way out. "And who cares what they say! Why does everyone think they know what's best for everyone else, when they don't even know what is right for them? I know what's best for me, and if that is you then lucky me! So what if we're twenty years apart!"

I hoped this would not turn into a discussion on the seriousness of our involvement, as I had yet to decide where it was headed. She lay there quietly for a moment, mulling over her thoughts on the matter and what her expectations were.

She lay silent for a moment and I had to know the thoughts brewing. “Why, what do you think?” I asked, tickling her elbow.

“I think we’re just fine. For now.”

“Good, me too.” Until later on when I changed my mind again, I thought.

“My dad used to tell me, Soosie, just follow your heart.” She paused. “And keep a map and a flashlight in your back pocket.”

“Soosie?” I saw an opening and hoped we were shifting gears.

“Oh, yeah, sorry. Soosie. It’s my family’s nickname for me.”

“Ooookaaaaay.”

“When I was a peanut, my mother would often say ‘so I see’ when she found something curious. I enjoyed how she said it, so I would often run around the house saying ‘so I see, so I see,’ and sometimes I would say it over and over again really fast, and it would come out ‘Soosie,’ so they made a joke of it and it stuck.”

I chuckled. “Cute.”

“Yeah I can be.”

I fell back, my head sinking softly into a pillow, my body free from all restraint and want of a mobility found in a younger version of myself. The ceiling fan above us began to turn on its own, although it was most certainly turned off, a detail I noticed in the midst of our circus act. I studied it and realized it was, in fact, turning and that the blades were throbbing.

Here we go, I thought.

In a flash the whole unit excused itself and separated from the ceiling, hurdling down towards us. I jumped as quick as possible, sure the fan would crush us, covering Claire with my body and snatched her up, sending us sprawling off the bed.

"What the—"

"Whoa, are you okay?" I asked, noting her shocked reaction. Even that face was a cute one.

"Yeah, fine, what was that about? If you wanted to wrestle, at least give me a head's up!"

"The fan..." I broke off, looking up to find my eyes had failed me again, the fan intact and secure. I sighed and apologized, crawling back up onto the bed, motioning for her to follow.

"Are *you* okay, Vey?"

"Not really...I don't know." I decided to tell her.

She looked worried, while a salad of disappointment and stupefied expectation hung from her face. The inevitability of time and chance lead me to believe she had endured a fair share of dead ends with the men in her life, considering the only relationship that ever truly works is the last one, if you're lucky, and have yet to become a widow. She wasn't married, and had no kids that I knew of, so I assumed they had all been roadblocks. Wait, unless she was, in fact, a widow. How would I bring that up? I wasn't sure, and assumed she thought I was another dead end. I quickly dispelled her fears.

"Nothing big, I don't think. Don't worry, I'm not psychotic or anything, but I've been having trouble with my eyes. It started the day we met. That's why I was panicked, it had nothing to do with my ears, I was just scared." I looked at her with intent, my face showing my sincerity and displeasure. "Things periodically change shape, dimensions shift, my depth perception becomes completely askew. Like right there, I thought the fan was falling on us."

"Whoa" she said, nudging closer and now rubbing my back. "You're not kidding are you?"

I shook my head, eyes on the fan, which started to shrink. I kept this minor detail to myself. "I wish I were."

"I'm so sorry. Have you seen a doctor?"

"Oh yeah, been there, done that. MRI, cat scan, blood work, you name it. Plus, I get really bad headaches and nausea in tandem. Sometimes before the ol' eyes start acting up, sometimes in the middle of it."

"So what is it?"

"Dunno. The doctors believe the headaches are the root, my sight a result." I shook my head. "I've tried a few meds, and finally one in particular gets rid of the headaches and the nausea, but nothing stops the illusions, they come and go at will."

"Oh my god, I'm so sorry, can I do anything?" She squeezed my hand and I hoped she would never let go.

I touched her face and grinned. "No, thank you...you're sweet. Just don't worry."

"How can I not?"

"I do enough for the both of us, just stay positive"

"I'll try."

"The worst part is that I have extreme difficulty painting. If I can't paint, I can't eat, and so forth, if you catch my drift. Oh and I'm afraid to drive. So thanks for picking me up, tonight. But painting...every time I try, the canvas changes shape, the colors change, I miss half the time and make a bloody mess. It's a very cruel joke." We both sat in silence for a minute or two, thinking it over.

I had nothing, but Claire's gears were clearly well lubricated.

"Well, I've seen some of your stuff, and it's pretty crazy to begin with. Who would know the difference between what you were trying to do an what actually came out?"

I raised a solitary eyebrow, and thinking she might be onto something, pictured the crap sitting in my basement.

"Like that there," she said, pointing to a wonderful mess of a piece I did hung across the room. "Did you do that one?"

"I did." Someone had once offered me ten thousand for it, but I knew my walls to be a more suitable home and informed them it had already been claimed for an undisclosed sum.

"And what is it?"

"It's what I see behind my eyelids when I close them."

"I love it, and I'm not just saying that...it's wild! But if you had told me it was what the ocean looks like when you open your eyes underwater I would have believed you too."

"What's your point?" I wasn't sure if I was offended or on the verge of enlightenment.

"Point is, maybe you should embrace it, go with it, instead of fighting it. Accept what you see and see what happens. What's the worst result? You paint a mess and no one likes it, or no one buys it, or maybe they do! Seems to me you've already made a pretty decent living out of your messes."

"Hey!"

"Hey yourself! Just calling it like I see it. You're obviously gifted, so see what else you can do with it, or better yet what *it* has planned with *you*. Just like in life, you never know what it has planned for you, so why close the doors so tight?"

I kicked her thought around and actually liked the idea. "You're pretty wise, Miss Claire."

"Eh, I'm getting there."

"So, have you ever been married?"

She laughed, shaking her head. "No, not yet. Someday hopefully"

I nodded. "Someday...good outlook."

"What other is there?"

"You ever think maybe it's not for you...maybe it's not

meant to be. We live in a culture, in a world, where everyone is assumed to be paired up at some point with *one* other person to spend forever with. Who says that's the answer?"

"Are you going to tell me polygamy is the answer?" she asked with a sarcastic laugh.

"No, no, no, just a different destiny. I don't know, I guess I think it sometimes, that maybe there isn't someone *just* right for me out there, or that maybe I'll never meet them even if it is my destiny, because a lot of it is just luck, and timing too. So to hang such lofty hopes in something which may never come to fruition, I don't know, it just seems like self-inflicted disappointment."

"It is, to a point, but I think there are thousands of just rights for everyone out there, and yes, if you're lucky, you'll meet one of them."

"Or else?" I asked.

"Or else what?"

My eyes lit up: "That's my point Claire, or else what? What do you do if you don't find one of them?"

"Well you never give up, for one. So unless you die, and can still think, you'll never know. If you know you are going to die and you haven't found someone, then you'll know. But by then you might be too old and tired to care anyway."

I shrugged. "Just seems like a long time to wait."

"If you call it waiting."

"What else is it?"

"Living."

"Living?"

"Yes living, living out your dreams, your fantasies, and everything in between. It's okay to have dreams, and it's okay if they don't all come true. It's the hope that if you continue to better yourself and be the best you that you can be, that some, if not all, of those dreams will see themselves realized."

"And what about having kids?"

"No thank you, we just met. Maybe someday," she said, catching her laughter in her hands.

I laughed with her, clutched her, and kissed her—hard. I wondered what the hell I was doing with this old lady, but ended up leg locked with her for the remainder of the night, unable, or willing, to let go.

8

After Claire's exit (she repeated her breakfast efforts, this time with French Toast), I napped a couple of hours, waking to a sea of white, my pillow having been impregnated with other pillows. I had woken other mornings in a state of illusion, yet this was the first time my pillow had been involved. From the moment she said it, I tried to embrace what I saw, instead of feeling inconvenienced and distraught and sorry for myself. I slapped the massive pillow several times, with an open hand and a grin, and took pride and pleasure in the fact that I now owned the world's largest. Guinness should be calling soon and I pictured the little black and white photo they would take.

As every other morning of my life, I ate, showered, and went to work. My commute was a short one: Fourteen unlit steps, the fourth and ninth which creaked from the strain. Staring at the canvas, whose shape bent in as if it were sucking air, or trying to fit into a snug pair of jeans, I decided to adopt a mind over matter approach. I set up as best I could and let my eyes follow the brush, tossing scarves of paint onto the white. At first the task seemed hopeless; I missed my target and the brush continually refused to cooperate. The canvas continued to shift and expand, then shy to a square the size of a matchbox. I moved closer, saddling my stool up close enough that I could follow the grains of the canvas to their roots. Now obnoxiously close, my face nearly pressed to the cotton board, I was better equipped to hit my mark but the broomstick I wielded blurred my view and I dropped the brush onto the floor. Frustrated and mocking the scene, I used my fingers to play with what I had already slapped on and the colors began to swirl, to dance, to make love to one another, and in a flash of electricity, redemption, and reward I moved in and out of a pellucid world where the sand of the shores, too, is water, where it thrives without pedantic grains, where I no longer needed brushes or borders or structure.

Stroke after stroke, I used all of my fingers and followed them with the awe and promise of a shooting star. Memories of yesteryear flashed in and out of the colors I mixed and I hated what I saw. I saw a version of me that smothered ants, cut traffic, and didn't return incorrect change. I saw lovers taken and hearts broken, promises made with no respect of their intended worth. I saw a life that had thrived on self-deceit and distaste for things wholesome and pure, strung out on a clothes line for all the neighbors to see. I tried to brush it all away, pretend it never happened, deny who I had become and absolve all my wrongdoings in a bloodbath of paint. It was then that I accepted what I saw and allowed a life which required trust and sacrifice and giving to take over. I succumbed to a being within, suppressed by years of torment and isolation from true experience. That being was freed and after climbing the walls it had detested for far too long, it traversed the shattered rim to look out and find, with a pair of eyes unused, there was hope yet.

A frenzied hour or two passed with my breath and heart maintaining thier excited pace, working to aid the discovery of a new land steeped in soil rich with possibility. Afraid to divert for the slightest of moments I tried not to blink, and after covering every checker-square inch of the board, I stepped back and stumbled over cans and bottles, falling back on my hands and hind, kicking up paint into the air onto my head, face, and the floor.

I laughed and laughed, sitting up to discover what I had just created. My studio looked as if a miniature paint factory exploded and no one cared to clean it up. The walls behind my stands bubbled, but the freshly buttered canvas stood eerily still, dimensions intact and its face a beautifully imperfect kaleidoscope of fireworks and sunsets. I was generally not thrown by my work, at times satisfied and confident in my efforts, but I had never composed anything with such an aftertaste. I looked down at my hands, an umber sauce saturating their lines, and realized I had just done my first finger painting in over thirty five years, the ligature weaving my insides tight with excitement.

Setting aside the gem, I hoped and prayed it was not a fluke, an aberration, and clumsily set up again. I repeated the same act for the next several hours, unaware of time and space. When I finally began to breathe again I found myself covered in oils. To the sink I hurried, rinsing my hands, hoping I had not washed away the new toy I had found. Thankfully my fears were belayed, and my heart took note, slowing with each passing breath.

Tears surfaced as I looked at what I had done, three solid works, small in size, but large in promise. Resting and drying, the images of each swaying and bending, the clematis of oil and prisms reaching to the clouds. I had not used a single brush, nor had I a moment of doubt or frustration, the extraordinary forms taking shape under the catharsis of my fingertips, working to build shelter from the rain for the weak and weary.

Hands on my hips, adding spots to my already paint addled jeans, I looked around the room at the disfigured furniture and the walls whose frescos were more surreal than their intended design, and I laughed. I had not seen things this way and I admitted the possibility I might never see things the same again.

Could it be this simple? No, I told myself, nothing is this easy. Life certainly isn't this easy. Or is it?

I was overcome with emotion, reminded of the essentials: my health, a roof over my head, food in my stomach. A soft kiss, a solemn sunset, a snow angel, blessings of the simplest sort. A new eye from within played a highlight reel of blissful moments I had experienced, yet failed to truly appreciate. I saw in those quick frames how the things I had treasured held no real value and that a much deeper, hidden beauty lie in so much more, apparently unseen when sleepwalking.

To Claire I owed my gratitude. She had forced the idea upon me, to absorb the bumps, drop the tumbrel, embrace the curves, and taste the tears of the rain. I must thank her. I had been avoiding the separation anxiety phone calls to her every four hours. I refused to be that guy. That guy has many different personalities but the one I speak of was a controlling, jealous, anxious buffoon. I would wait, a day or two even, there was no rush to be in. Plus, there was much to be seen and done at home.

Ten wondrous hours of finger painting passed before my efforts gave in to the needs of hunger and thirst, and I hated having to waste my time eating, afraid I might lose the place I was in. When you are on the merry go round you don't ever want to get off. Stopping is okay, different heights bring different views of the neighboring horsies, but after enough rotations you start to wonder if each go around is the last and if not, then the next one, and so on. I was afraid to stop spinning. Some might call it a zone, but to me it was a free place where there was no judge, or jury, only imagination and belief, a place, anyplace really where the things that melt your eyes with their beauty sparkle in the lights they were born to.

I was anxious and felt incredibly alive from the events

that had taken place in my basement. What do I do now? I could continue to paint through the night, through the days, but I felt a burning curiosity torching my insides, curious to see the world. I still wasn't driving, so I could not go very far, thus the streets I had called home for so many years would have to suffice. I did not know what I was looking for but I knew that whatever it was it was out there somewhere. Something alive and radiating that pulled me out into the world to follow it's footsteps. It wasn't a particular landmark or a bustling city or sanctuary I sought, but merely the vitality of everything that amassed all which I had missed when I thought I knew what I didn't really know. It was getting late, but it was also a Saturday, there was no such thing as late, for even when late came it was still referred to as "early morning".

I showered and watched the colors fall from my hands and arms, swimming lazy circles around my feet before succumbing to the waterfall of their deaths and I wondered if I shouldn't try toe painting as well. I thought about drying and trying, but decided I would never be known as the foot painter. Fingers were one thing.

9

It takes five minutes and forty four seconds to fill my bathtub with hot water. I can run to the end of the shore from my front stoop and back in an hour and fifty five minutes. Average time to wash and dry my hands: thirty seconds. Five seconds to tie my shoe. Twelve to close up the button fly on my jeans and another fourteen to put on my belt. Total jeans and tee shirt dressing time: fifty five seconds.

I time and measure everything, hopping from one thing to the next. There is no in-between for me. Only this and next. A mad fellow once accused me of not respecting time, but I feel I may give it more than it deserves. So much so, that I miss life, busy hurrying to complete each task before me to start and finish the next one by the most efficient means. If there is a shortcut I will find it, an easier way I will use it. A limit, I will adjust and set it. Idle time is wasted time and unproductive time is exactly that.

With a sad, curious look back, I could see that my organization of each day into little blocks built nothing but a wall which held out the usher of time: chance.

There is chance in every facet of our day. From the chance that there will be enough milk left in the carton to fill a bowled selection of cereal to the chance that the hot water will be flowing properly when attempting to clean the same emptied bowl, there stands a variable amount of chance in every transpiration we experience. For years I did well to eliminate any anxiety or thought of such seemingly safe randomness by placing everything in its cubby, dependent upon an absolute truth governing it. In the end, the element of surprise was missing from my periodic table and I had relatively complete control of all of the outcomes in my life. And where had that gotten me? Lost. Lost in a world where things really aren't what they seem.

10

Pay attention you fool. This I told myself, stepping outside the door as if setting foot on foreign soil, the excitement of what was to come spraying my insides like an effervescent mist. How would the air smell? How would the light feel on my skin? The first time on the west coast I felt the warm, salted air the moment I set foot off the plane and the sun's warmth was coated with an extra something, as if it, too, hated to waste its rays elsewhere. If it was all in my head then the joke is on me, but I recall the same phenomenon happening in Vegas, Mexico and Wyoming. Yes, Wyoming. Don't ask. Oh very well then, it was a fishing trip. A whim of a trip, as I have no honest knowledge of where the poles I bought are today.

I hadn't researched what was to come, as I might do upon heading to Australia, say, or Egypt, careful to find establishments that catered to phony, rude, bewildered Americans. I had a fairly decent idea what I might find in the city which raised me, so I didn't need a three-leafed pamphlet highlighting the dining scene, or the public restrooms, or the wind addled statues that spoke of a history I would never appreciate, but I did need to see for myself the life behind every face and breathe the current that had passed me by for so long.

When you set your life on program, an endless series of predictable moments fall in step, and you, the programmer, lose peripheral, as well as the notion to inhale, to embrace, to appreciate. I cannot know for certain how long I had been riding that horizontal escalator, as the moment it began I apparently was oblivious to its taking my arm and leading the way to the ensuing waltz. The needle had just slipped and the dance came to an abrupt halt.

My feet shuffled along the dusty sidewalk, my jeans hung low on my hips, gently draping it with each step. My feet felt light, and my smile reflected their enjoyment. The white collared shirt I wore kept me warm against the cool breeze kissing my face. The colors were rich, even the gray, weathered stone of the townhouses that lined my street spoke up in the dark afternoon of October.

My thoughts ran thick, a syrup of ease and assurance that stood to remind me of the power that lie in positivity. I politely shouldered out any ideas which sought to weigh upon my delight. If something pressing should demand attention or an emergency should arise, I would be ready for whatever the task, but with the exception of either, I would continue to revel in, and marvel at, the grin I was so easily able to procure, and substantiate, for as long as I could.

I was floating with carefree determination, walking without a time limit or a necessary purpose, just happy to be alive. Good for me, I thought, and enjoyed the new shoes I felt I was wearing. I studied the faces of passers by, noting their sadness and unresponsiveness. I guessed the age of everyone I saw and wondered where in their progressive time line they stood.

The things we are led to believe need and shall come, well, they happen differently to people and by varying sunsets, or sometimes not at all: marriage, children, retirement, hair that grows in the middle of your forehead. Sure, they all arrive eventually for most, but why were we all so affixed to the time limits associated with each? I thought back to Claire's ideas on mortality.

I crossed shadows with a bearded man I deemed to be in his mid fifties and compared the imagined state of affairs I placed upon him with the realities of my own. I decided he was about fifty five, and married with two kids out of college, yes, that sounded about right to me. Perhaps he would soon be a grandfather for the first time, or eyeing an early retirement, having put in over thirty years at his current job.

Looking at my situation, my pushpin was nowhere near this man's on the map—my clear pin unnoticed with a quick glance compared to this man's un-plucked green one. I wasn't married, had no kids and had no real retirement plan. I thought I would paint till I died and truly felt that until this point in my life I might have been looking at life through the wrong peek hole. Nevertheless, I wasn't jealous of this man or downtrodden, but amused that life had no supposed course, aside from the winding road that brought birth to death. The endless side roads in between were mine to traverse, and I refused to let the obstacles that had scarred me along the way to detract from the place I was in. I was still the sculptor of it all, I could make it an ashtray, or a coffee mug, or I could opt to put down the clay and knit myself a quilt with which to pull up to my neck and keep me snug and warm. I knew not what was to come, whether I would marry, if children would bounce on my knee, or if my retirement would mean bagging groceries at the Saver Mart. And that was okay. Not knowing every outcome was okay.

I came upon a boy no older than ten, clumsily making his way in the same direction as myself on a skateboard, and I thought to myself that I could take up skateboarding at the tender age of forty two and assuredly be looked at as immature and silly. Fine, be that as it may, there was nothing but my own disinterest and ego to stop me. What was really preventing me from doing anything I pleased? If I chose to turn around, go home and pack all of my things and relocate to a shack in the mountains, who could stop me? Who would care?

I continued to seek out scattered faces and determine their worth. I found more sadness than I had expected, and wondered how many were tied to the back of the same bumper I grew to know so well for so long, the rusted trailer hitch masquerading as life support. I was now in the drivers seat for the first time, piloting the heap of metal without the need to hotwire it, for it appeared as though I had fetched the right key.

I flung open the door to Downtown Records, our city's lone music store, and was excited just to be alive. The little bell that hung from the doorway rang with a spry jingle as if to certify my glee. I made my way to the vinyl, seven rows mixed with new and used LPs, and dug in. I wasn't searching for anything in particular, just something to jumpstart my new life. It is amazing, I thought, how a single second can pass and instantly dreams can be realized or crushed or imagined. The impulsive itch tickling my feet felt like spring's arrival, the excited, untitled song of a bird gracing the fresh morning air.

I found an old Bob Dylan album with one slightly worn corner and took note of its presence while I continued to flip, the patter of the jackets meeting a welcome tune. I couldn't remember the last time I felt such grateful joy in such a simple task. Flip, flap, flop. More albums, more memories of good times and bad, lovers and strangers and in between. The ticking pleasure-bomb inside me grew louder and I grew more anxious. Before my inventory was complete I decided it would be Dylan, forgoing a couple of rows, and plucked the winner from its resting place. The cover spoke to me, and I imagined myself wearing the velvety violet jacket he donned on the cover.

The tall, laid back clerk accepted my bouncy arrival,

referring to me as "bro." He asked if I wanted a receipt, and I thought to ask him if he wanted his paycheck, since these little pieces of paper we give out are of such little importance to him.

"Please." I said, keeping my thoughts to myself.

"Okay, bro, you got it!" He seemed far from sad, and I remembered being twenty two; there was little to be sad about.

I tried to take my time going home, yet the serum coursing through my limbs had other plans. My legs were strong and my vision could not settle on anything for more than a blink. Was anything truly possible? That was how it felt, and something so simple as learning to paint, to create, to feel—as if the first time—was all it took. That and this little annoying eye thing. Oh and this little not-so-annoying little creature named Claire. They might have helped too.

The sounds that played in the background were a perfect soundtrack. The hiss of a bus, the clink of glass and dish from the open back door of a restaurant, the jumbled notes from songs playing in nearly every direction. I listened to all the ideas exchanging hats in my head. What things had I missed through blankets of rain? How much experience had I forgone in exchange for meaningless trophies and a warped ego?

Certainly my entire approach towards relationships had gotten me nowhere, and I hoped it wasn't too late for a middle-aged man to finally make one work. Was it? I told myself it wasn't, and wondered if Claire was the answer. It was too soon to tell, I argued, so why was I so eager to pounce the bell? There were plenty of women I would still meet, and date, and if I were fortunate enough, one might convince the cynics holding court in my heart that all the others were a waste of time.

But wasn't that the same tale I told myself since becoming a man? The same excuse which would afford me further time to fritter away? What was different now?

I could suddenly see, that's what. I saw before only that which I desired to see, that which I thought was important, the superficial scrape of a much deeper wound, but how much had I missed along the way? How many opportunities to laugh, to cry, to be alive in the river of life with it's wild, foamy ideas. How many women had I dismissed or thrust away based on my one track mind? Should I try to reconcile any of them? I knew this idea was absurd, considering I made it a point to end all of my relationships in such a manner that a lingering, awkward friendship would not remain to haunt me or my sleep.

A short list of names scrolled across my mind, ending with Melanie, and my smile shrunk until the sudden screeching of tires pulled me from the discouraging thread. I looked up to see two cars, stopped side by side in the center of the intersection before me, thin wisps of smoke streaming from their tailpipes. I scanned the block and tried to determine who was in the wrong, but I could not figure how the cars got into the position they had. They were saddled up as if waiting for more cars to join so the man on the motorcycle could jump them to the delight of a roaring crowd...

My question was answered when the large driver of the black pickup decided to open his door and verbally abuse the woman driving the red compact sedan with one leg still in his truck, the other hovering over the space between he and the open door which he used to sturdy his arm. I figured his assault was certainly a wise decision, as the owner of the little car was assuredly looking forward to constructive feedback on the incident. I was curious if she had any wounds he might care to salt while he was at it.

"Off with your head!" yelled the ungrateful woman with her window half rolled.

Off with your head? I literally spit laughing as I did not see this retort coming.

"Off with your head!" Again she cried out in response to the tall man's assault. I could not tell what he was saying, but I knew it wasn't kind. I also could not help but stare and enjoy the pointless exchange. Who didn't enjoy a good fracas?

"Off with your head!" Apparently someone needed new material, and I wondered if she knew beheadings were no longer custom. Before I could witness the riveting conclusion, I was struck unexpectedly by my condition, as I grew to call it, when I scratched my nose and found my hands enlarged for the first time in weeks. I could not recall them growing to such forms since day one, and I was alarmed for a quick moment, then relieved and laughing when I imagined the players in the traffic scene running from the man with the freakish hands, hurdling towards them as if to swat them like pesky flies.

No longer interested in the outcome, I checked the sky for any messages, and turned left towards my castle, shaking my head with a chuckle, clown hands by my side. If only they knew how ridiculous they looked, and how many more important things lie await to expend their energy on. Ahh, life was grand. People were fighting and I was smiling. If I got home and found a fire had diminished it all to rubble, would I still be? Probably not at first, but within seconds I thought I would. The house, and all its internal organs, would surely grow back.

The soft, intermittent crackle coming out of the speakers gently caressed my ears and I doubted gravity could hold me down for much longer. Lost in a smirking daze for over two hours, I rose only to flip the record I had bought every half hour. Up to flip one last time and hungry again, I made my way into the kitchen, whose counters still bore their constructed dimensions, tore open a box of thin spaghetti and dropped the contents into the bubbling pot I had readied. I hung my face over the steam rising from the pot for a few seconds, my skin sucking in the warmth and moisture. The grin on my face left subtle lines that faded.

I was never enrolled, and hence never served, in the

armed forces, yet to watch me eat one might think so. I had never appreciated the art of chewing your food with patience, instead opting to put as much as my cheeks would hold on temporary standby for swallowing, while my molars quickly cut the deposits into more manageable pieces for my throat as if they were being timed. I thought I had always enjoyed the process to the fullest, until I slowly twirled my pasta to Dylan's Idiot Wind and chewed each bite as though it might be my last. Starch had never tasted better, although I had yet to try most of the nearly three hundred and fifty shapes it took on.

Amazing, I thought, how for so many years I looked at each tidbit of my existence as something I needed to conquer, to devour, to rule. Irradiated, I decided to take my time, not solely with eating, but with everything. Brushing my teeth, taking a shower(which I had previously cut down to four and a half minutes), folding laundry, all these things and more I now saw as tiny blessings, and not chores whose untimely interruption took away from my day's enjoyment. I embraced everything I could think of, and with such care, grateful to have the opportunities and options that I did.

In the days to come I took more walks about town, ignoring the clocks, using the sun as my guide, and even managed to visit my parents resting place without shame or overwhelming shapes to stop me. I had been harboring the guilt of blissfully eating pancakes from a woman old enough to be my mother while they were upstairs playing hide-and-go-seek in the clouds. No longer a weight I dragged along, my well-overdue visit ensured me that the love they had for me truly was eternal, as they had always promised it was, and I could feel it enriching me wherever I went, with each precious step I took.

I spoke to more and more people, but more importantly, I listened. Never having done so without a motive, I now found the joy people gained from speaking into a caring ear with a smile to support it. For years I had spoken only to hear myself talk and listened only to await my turn again. Now I felt humbled by my own voice, realizing the world would go on without me, perhaps even for the better. Being hard on myself was nothing new, but for once I had unbiased substance to back it up. Again, I traveled back to all that I had said and done and wished I could erase so many words, take the books I filled with my tireless banter, and burn them all.

I had yet to properly thank Claire for her help. We hadn't spoken in a couple of days, I busy in my work and my new head, and she with her work and night school classes. Only Claire, I thought, would still be trying to further herself at that age, whatever that age was. Everything she said and did seemed to tickle me. I hated being tickled until now, and I wondered if I might enjoy cream cheese too. I doubted it.

A full moon graced the autumn sky at twilight one day when I reached her from home and told her I had a kiss for her, better delivered in person.

"Oh really?" she said with the sweet of candy in her voice, "And who says I'm ready to take that step, mister painter man? I'm just a respectable little lady being courted by an old man in a big, big world."

I laughed, she always had me on the verge of one, too. "Well, Miss, then I can only hope to enjoy the pleasure of your company, and pray that kisses might come in good time!"

"Hmmm. Okay hotshot, I sup*pose* I can squeeze one in for you. I'm booked solid, so you're lucky I have a thing for hallucinating painters." She was just getting off work and said she would be at the park within the hour, so I should come by to meet a few people special to her. I did not stop to think the offer over and find reason to avoid the social exercise, as my glee had overridden most of my incendiary thoughts.

Fed, showered, and clad in my running gear, I set out, the size and shape of the world no longer a concern, and half-hoped for the periodic mind trickery to confront me on my run, to find where it might take me.

A chilled breeze made way through my face, continuing on behind me its eternal journey to everywhere and nowhere, never knowing whose lips it might graze or whose lungs it might fill. Several blocks away from my house the earth held its form. I searched every car, every façade, every mobile body, every fragment of civilization for its twisted step brother, but found the tempered air held the world in check, as new expressions spawned on faces, the blood that ran hot and thick within simmered to the calls of a new season. The birds gave flight, working steadily to prepare their eventual descent to more accommodating climates, being sure to investigate the neighborhoods for any last trace of treasure.

My legs fought me that day, and as any little sister would do, my lungs filed protest as well. They demanded a day of sedentary compliance, but it was too late for such compromise. I had given my word to meet Claire, and thankfully it was still true in someone's ears.

Upon entering the park I decided to walk, staying close to the water, its swaying boats frowning that day under the overcast sky, knowing their days to be numbered. Before long, the salt water soak they enjoyed would soon be over, displaced with suffocating tarps and garages that would imprison their unseen winters. Several kayaks slit the water with grace, trying their best to prolong their use and avoid menial solitude. Theses vessels would have a short break compared to the boats', for their masters dismissed the pain of cold's hand, which otherwise stood as winter's strong fist upon the earth.

With the tables in sight, I picked up my pace and ran by, allowing myself an escape with a wave if Claire wasn't there by chance. My instincts held serve as when I coasted by, I did not see Claire, but did see some familiar faces, and some new ones, too. I was greeted with warm smiles and flirty invitations from a pair of twenty-somethings, the apparent grandchildren of the bunch. I did my best to seem flattered and uninterested, mindful of the jealousies some women possessed should Claire be within range, watching. Something had changed within me and I decided that such harmless flirtations weren't worth the price, and I hadn't the funds, regardless.

I forced my legs to obey and together we encompassed the beautiful, grayed shoreline as we had many times before. I saw the lines and the hues in every leaf, in every twig that lay scattered without proper burial, in every jilted cigarette shrunken and passed out drunk, in every man, woman, and child whose life brought noise to the circus that was populated Earth, in the motley of injustice that stood at the forefront of the universe for space tabloid headlines to exploit. Through my viewfinder, I saw the microbes that lived independently and simultaneously with each other to strike down any notion of obscurity or death. They would not be denied the sun's nourishment or the moon's goodnight kiss.

To the north the path I continually beat on came to an end in the form of a miniature cul-de-sac, with four innocent benches circling the pavement. Beyond them the green of the park continued for several dozen yards, giving way to the Park Department's Headquarters and then the spacious two mile stretch of homes and private docks admired by anyone who possessed a sense of taste. The northern part of town housed a great many wealthy, and the gang wars fought with the south side commenced annually at the town's Appreciation Days (a summer weekend of carnival games, greasy food, and face painting), in the form of the north-versus-south potato sack races.

I slowed at an open bench and sat atop it's back, my lean, thin figure lank from the exertion and wet with perspiration. I looked across the river where our neighbors to the east stood, the small city of smoke sputtering industries and endless warehouses. I checked my fingernails for dirt, found none, and doubted they could say the same across the water. The blue collar life would never be for me, and I instantly wondered who the hell I thought I was, and why I was so damn special.

Searching the sky for a trace of blue, I sighed, and found nothing in which to rejoice. The clouds owned the sky that day, refusing to remove their shroud. The crystalline ceiling which always seemed to hold court in our town would have to be patient while the mirth of the dark sky ran its course. I had generally found myself impatient on such days, wishing the end, the renewal of hours, for a new sky on hand, bright with promise and infinity. As common as this is, I did not see myself as suffering from any contrived condition needing periodic courses of therapy and medication, as many others had, excusing their foul moods and generally negative disposition on the weather and lack of celestial light. No, I merely chalked it up to my affinity for the sun and bright heavens, and thought it a simple human condition, as shivers are on a fiercely cold day.

The water, a modest stone's throw away from where I sat, rustled anxiously, the wind feathering its top layer. I thought perhaps the following year I would purchase a boat, the seclusion of my house having recently forced me to examine my leisure activities more carefully. I had never been much of a fan of things nautical, a peculiar quality for someone having grown in size and stature in its shadow. I adored the tranquility of it, from a short distance, yet in its vast pool I had always been lost, displaced. Looking out at it now I imagined I could peacefully reside on a boat and revel peacefully in the current, the hot soup in my head spilling out my ears.

Back around again, I found the same figures sharing words and faces and gestures around the chess tables. With the music in my ears muffling the sounds, and no sign of Claire, the matching pair of pretty girls giggled and called something aloud to me which I could not make out, yet returned with a wave and feigned laughter. I worried little of Claire's absence, which was most likely due to a work issue. I figured she had called my cell phone(which I had left at home when I ran) or that she had already come and gone.

In no hurry, I walked most of the way home, passing the liquor store which had led to much of my recent pain. I palindrome I. The relaxed air within the city walls cooled my sweat until it evaporated to a place I guessed was filled with odd socks and pens. I reflected on the days to come, the new love I was ready to spoon feed, and the New Year's finger painting show certain to be different from all the others. The tide had shifted. What I thought to be a curse had manifested as a gift. I loved gifts.

Safely home, I called Claire and left a message, apologized for missing her, unsure if it was any fault of my own. Hours later, not hearing from her, I called again to make certain nothing had happened. The recent befalling of those within close proximity to me sprouted fear and worry and I tried to shake the thoughts, but it was hard not to entertain their flirtations.

For dinner I ate tender ziti the apparent size of cigars, topped with a modicum of sauce, and I enjoyed it, while in my mouth they felt normal size. It became a new challenge—I had always enjoyed challenges—to solve the riddles my eyes had asked me. Watching television and using the computer were still obstacles and I had difficulty surmounting, while the prehensile worlds in my books fought their lettered destinies, but I was able to adapt, wading through the ink shelves that shaped their symbols. My obsessive sense of cleanliness took a concerted dip as I often spilled water over the rims of glasses and shuffled food on and off plates with the grace of a three legged dog. After a while, I didn't care; a joke was a joke; even when knocking things over the old groans of yesterday had slowly turned to chuckles. All in all I managed considerably well, and accepted the occasional folly. A joke was a joke, with the exception of the deadly shin-to-coffee-table confrontation.

I returned a good many phone calls to those who had been trying to make a connection for the past month or so. “Deep in my work” was what I said, and apologized for my absence and aloofness. This was nothing new of course, my sporadic fade from the exocentric lines of communication. Sometimes this social exclusion lasted days while other stretches eclipsed months. I allowed no guilt to seep into my veins for the blatant ignorance I displayed, hiding behind my work and the walls it helped to erect.

Those close to me knew me well enough to excuse my disconnect, although being close to me was a concept of great relativity. I cannot say if anyone has actually ever been truly close to me, the series of gates leading from the outside world to the depths of my being continually having their locks changed.

After my parents death I did a splendid job of pronouncing my fierce and unrelenting resolve, attempting to prove to the world that it mattered not that the love and support which had encircled me wherever I stood had evaporated in the most oppressive of heat waves.

Always active, my folks were a three-dimensional, thirty minute public service announcement for a healthy lifestyle. Up before my alarm clock stabbed me with its announcement of another school day, the two of them ran the crust of the river and back every day, as I have too since their passing. Until then, I thought it a silly ritual, saw no pleasure being gained from it, and shook my head laughing every morning when they came bouncing in the front door to find me shoveling sugar-infested cereal into my numb and barely functioning head.

"Good morning, sunshine," my mother would call out, the smile in her voice highlighting the warm sentiment.

"Heya' champ," father would echo, and I often wondered if he rose with the birds just to make her happy. He would squeeze blood from rock to make her beam, and sometimes it sickened me, although I understood and knew that he, too, was of equal nobility in her eyes.

Running, swimming, camping, sailing. If you could think it and declare it healthy they incorporated it into their lives, a solid effort to outlast the gods. If not for the hole, they might have triumphed. I, on the other hand, lacked the coordination to enjoy their lust for mobility. You should have seen me try to jump rope.

I was grateful they didn't push their hobbies upon me, content that my art would lead me to all the fulfillment I would want and need. Looking back, I wished they had nudged harder or dragged me to overcome my distaste for the outdoor life and join them. I have since carried the idea that a show of effort on my part may have saved them from their plight had I been there to call for help, or play the fall guy myself.

On the third Saturday of a new year, I was fifteen and three eights, and while my friends were up early for their basketball games, I was mixing paint; I shot like a girl and threw like one with no arms. That crisp, gray, winter morning, the floors cold on my bare feet, my mom and dad spent the early part gearing up for a day of hiking, picnicking, and kissy-face. They hadn't bothered to ask me to join them, merely informing me of their plans—void of their destination—knowing of my consistent disinterest in where they planned on scraping their shins and dirtying their palms in an effort to reach the top of a hill they would eventually have to descend. They knew I would take happy refuge in my own realities and colors, avoiding wind-burned cheeks and frozen toes.

The car was ticketed twice before the plates were run, two weeks later, and the papers later enjoyed grating law enforcement of the small town where they had gone hiking, over and hour and a half north of my poster-filled room. A long drive, I thought, to merely walk up and down. Into a literal pit of death they fell, and froze, covered for days by newly detached leaves and branches the winds showered upon them. To this day I have yet to hear a reasonable explanation of the hole's existence or formation, too big for any animal to have burrowed, and if manmade, for what purpose I know not.

I had slept in their bed the second night they did not come home, the lingering scents of lavender and shaving cream a reminder of their being. My aunt moved in after a week of crashing on our couch, nothing yet revealed of my folks whereabouts, and I enjoyed the extra pulse in the house. She had lived in a run down apartment—above a barber shop—with poor heat, and seemed humbled by her arrival. I am sure her brother's disappearance diminished any pleasure she might have normally taken in the upgrade.

Aunt Helena was an odd gal, I often thought, but really, she was, regardless of what I thought. I had never know her to have a boyfriend, or girlfriend, let alone a husband, or a wife, nor did she mother any children. I never knew her to have much of anything, always working part time jobs in antique stores and small craft shops as if to certify the old saying, "another man's junk...". She found peace in the quiet of silence and hid from a world too busy to find the volume knob.

After their stiff and huddled bodies were discovered, I found myself alone in the world except for Helena, which at most times was very much the same. She hardly engaged in conversation, preferring to spend her spare time (in strong supply) toiling over unnecessarily large jigsaw puzzles. The guestroom was bare to begin with, so we set up a large card table for her to waste time on, or so I saw it. I helped her a few times, trying to fit pieces of soft blue into a vast and endless cardboard sky. I couldn't find the entertainment value in it, wishing for the precious minutes—filled with yawns and budding headaches—back. Our conversations were always short, and yet to a pleasant point; she had managed to adopt the same positive spin on things my parents had embodied, and I accepted that she was indeed family.

I once asked her, minutes before my senior prom, if she had any advice for me. It was my first date with Ann Coulter, the cheerleader who would later in life be arrested for smuggling animal tranquilizers into the country from Mexico. Funny where wrong turns can take you. At the time of the prom she was not a practicing smuggler, not that I knew. Aunt Helena looked at me over her glasses, sitting low on her nose which pointed at the covered bridge in need of another thirty or so of its dispersed pieces to be placed. She stood up and put her hands on her hips, smiling such a pretty smile; I often thought it a waste of a good smile, since so few got to see it. "Veymont Addison, don't be afraid to let the world see who you are, especially those girls! If they aren't smitten with someone as charming and special as yourself, then that's not the kind of girl you want anyway. Oh and don't get any of 'em pregnant." She grabbed me in the most affectionate of bear hugs and squeezed me with all she had, crushing the white carnation pinned to my lapel.

I found the advice strangely helpful, coming from someone I imagined to be asexual and immotile. Nevertheless, I appreciated her care and thankfully did not impregnate anyone. It wasn't often that I asked her for advice, feeling that I knew more about the outside world and public relations than she did. It was also my age speaking; kids think they know everything, and in the end know nothing.

Years passed, as they have a habit of doing. I ate, slept,

studied, and painted. Life goes on. Still in art school, I had my first solo show, and moved out a month later at age twenty one. I made enough money in a week to support me for the next year, and while I was learning to become an overly motivated soldier of consumption, my aunt continued to stay in the house we would eventually sell. My parents savings had covered the bills for months beyond my departure, and Helena could have stayed there forever as far as I was concerned. After we said goodbye to the house I was raised in, she wanted the entire profit from the sale to go to me, but I insisted we split it, knowing my fortune would come, happy to pay the old piker back while the chance was there.

The lines of communication between the two of us sagged in the years to come: I, immersed in my freedom and selfishness, and Helena in her simplicity. The token holidays we exchanged cards and offsetting gift checks, but rarely did we visit one another. Our shared quiet prevented awkward barbeques from sprouting up randomly. I didn't mind. I made my own happiness, my own decisions, and let the painful memories of family and yesteryear fade with the sun on a tight lipped horizon. Aunt Helena passed from stomach cancer eleven years after I moved out and to this day I still detest jigsaw puzzles.

11

Apparently there was fault on my part in Claire's eyes. I did not receive a return call or so much as a polite smoke signal. Five days passed, and I reluctantly accepted the end. I was not completely sold, but the signs were clear. Silence can be very loud. I hoped for some strange, believable explanation to ease my disappointment, but unfortunately it did not come. I was the punch line.

Her exodus was surprising, yes, yet from the beginning I harbored the belief our affair might be short lived. Most of my relationships have been short lived, so I rarely have reason to believe they will survive any great duration. Perhaps she held those very same expectations and the newfound, overwhelming affinity I felt was one-sided. It seemed as though she shared the bond, but I had to admit it was entirely possible that I was just a naïve boy falling for the older woman, who was much wiser and respectable in her age.

I was disappointed by her defection. Not a single note from her voice, music I truly wished to hear, yet accepted being without, since I had something else to bury myself in: my art, which had found new direction. I continued to finger paint, the surreal ideas swimming in endless color and riding the sound of the hands and pursed breaths helping to shape their spines. I did not need love, I told myself. I did not need companionship, another body in which to confide, to exhaust my emotions, my fears, my ecstasies. The weak needed that, and I was not weak. I could carry on and soldier on and play on. Nothing would thwart my efforts, most certainly not the lack of a female counterpart; I wouldn't be searching for any pickup games of Russian Roulette. Although short lived, I yearned to, and enjoyed, being alone, as I did when any seemingly incurable negativity lingered in my world, including matters of the heart. This began as a teen, as the hours I spent painting and my parents' eventual absence left me alone more often that not for years, and I found that riding solo had its virtues, and unaccountability was one of them. Twenty five years later I had long since mastered the art of seclusion and felt responsible for nothing until my eyes saw differently for me.

Halloween a week away, I was confident my newfound skills would carry me to the tippity come the first of the year. The strangeness of the recent months had been worth their price, and a peculiar sensation highlighted my creativity; I began not to think in dollar signs, but in smiles. Whatever that old woman had done to me, its effects would not rub off no matter how desperately the ideals of a me from chapters ago tried. I was anew, my world was anew, my work was anew, and I could not have been more grateful. Or anew, in case I failed to mention it.

I got serious, deciding to compose pieces large enough to fill the emptiness of an entire wall. These would be time consuming, but with no schedule to adhere to, and no love life to speak of, the disappearing act could continue. For the first time, however, I felt and realized just how forsaken I was, how the connections in life I made never amounted to anything except paved roads that turned to dust and sunsets that shut off with the flick of a switch once their destinies were realized and brought to fruition for even the briefest of moments. The happiness I had felt in recent weeks was due to an appreciation for things real and derived from deep within the confines of a place devoid of light for far too long.

The storefronts that had marked the rest of my life proved to be nothing more than lipstick and false contacts—smoke and mirrors which had fueled my walk through the days thus far. I now had no choice but to see things from different heights, with different shapes and sizes, my eyes had seen to that, but also because the abyss which I had trudged down into so willingly had cut off the light from above and promised salvation from the fire at the bottom that damned my previous existence with each step.

I missed Claire and the safety in which she wrapped me in. I missed following the words that left my mouth, hoping they fell upon her ears with soft hands and warm embraces. Most words before had parted my lips with a return token expected, a pre-measured angle I had recorded; with Claire I only wished to open her lips in the form of a smile and fill the balloons that kept her afloat with an air that never thinned or complained of the ribbon tied round its neck. I asked for nothing in return, seeking only to fill her with the warm intimations bubbling inside my heart.

I decided to call her one last time and apologize again for whatever wrong I had done. I had never been one to dole out sorries for much; the world was filled with enough wrong that all the regret and apology would never assure its restitution be delivered. I excused my arrogance based on a numbers game; I was just a microcosm of the energy that spun the earth, insignificant and unnoticed and my relationships were bound by little adhesive, allowing my actions little consequence, prolonged effect, or strain on my conscience.

Confused by my situation with Claire, I tried to understand where I had gone wrong. I was surprised by the anguish I felt over someone I had known for such a brief period of time, and better yet, so unlike what I was normally attracted to. I was never one to cry over broken connections—copper phone lines were always subject to corrosion, and I would be okay.

I rested on the fact that I had a lifetime to find someone to share my misery with, or perhaps not at all. I enjoyed the variety of women I came across and spent time with, and was truly unsure if I could love anyone enough to count down eternity with; I had a hard enough time getting along with myself!

Still, the rise and fall of my affair with Claire left confusion at my doormat. I replayed all of my actions and all the things I said for nearly every day since we met. I thought I had proceeded at a safe enough speed, careful not to profess anything desperate, or allow things to get carried away, or display any desire to be involved in anything void of possible attachments. I thought time was on my side in that developing, short lived blossom. Apparently not.

I had accepted her outward appearance, and the age she showed. She was beautiful regardless of what her birth certificate read, and she made me unquestionably happy. I accepted the fact that I might not have forever with her, whatever that actually meant, but whatever time I had would be enough, and I had to see it through, see what could be, see what it had planned for me. I accepted the fact that I couldn't have kids with her, and that if by some crazy chance we did end up together, we would have to channel our love in another direction, or maybe not (the option of adoption stood available, something I had never until then given considerable thought to).

Immersed in unresolved thoughts, emotions, and more

questions than I could find answers to, I had let my standards go, or rather my unfair expectations. I saw Claire for *who* she was, and not what I wanted her to be, and she was intelligent, amusing, charming, beautiful, and so much more! I was amazed, proud that I could get past the physical, and the age, and the unknown, and see her in the light that shone soft and tender above her. A sense of accomplishment accompanied my desire to show her sides of me previously held in captivity. I deserved someone like her, I thought—I hoped. I had secretly known I was capable of loving in a way that was selfless and unconditional and even if I should find it would not be with her, I hoped she might further provide insight on how, or in which direction to look, but either way I knew that following her was the path intended.

Luck was either on my side, or curious to see what I was made of, as Claire answered my call, her languid tone not in the least encouraging.

"Yes?"

"Hi, It's Veymont." I assumed she knew this, but felt it necessary to disclose.

"I know, Vey. Can I help you?"

"I just haven't heard from you, I was worried something had happened."

"Worried? Oh, I'm sure." Ouch. "Look, I don't have time for silly games, I made that clear from the beginning."

"Games?" I looked at my tiny phone, in disbelief it could play such strange words in my ear. "What—"

"No, don't! It's okay if you don't want to be seen with me, that's fine. I know we didn't discuss the age difference in great detail, but I thought you weren't too concerned. You've made it abundantly clear you are, so I'm making it easy for you. Now don't make it difficult for me. Please."

"Claire, I'm sorry if I gave you that impression. I admit I have, well, *had,* some concerns, but like I said before, it doesn't matter just yet. In fact, come to think of it, it doesn't matter at all. I don't even know what I did to piss you—"

"Don't know? Are you serious? You really are a trip! You think you can just call me up and I'll come running back to your bed like one of your little play things, naïve and impressed by the big shot artist? I'm sure there are plenty of young girls out there who will allow themselves to be strung along and kept behind the glass for you to break when your pleasure needs present themselves, but I am also quite sure, Veymont, that you are well aware that is *far* from me!" She had me on the ropes and I still had no idea why she forced me there.

I remained silent while I thought of something to fix this mess, but she followed up:

"I like you, Vey, I *liked* you—you seemed real to me. But if that's who you really are, then you have prove it, you can't just say things and fail to back them up with some substance, some compassion...some decency!"

"That is me! And perhaps you are right, it wasn't always me. I don't know what you've heard or who you're listening to, but I am real, in fact, since I met you, Claire, I'm more real than ever before! Please let me show you!" I couldn't believe the words leaving my mouth. I was reminded of a conversation I had with Melanie before watching a truck wipe out a row of cars in front of my house.

"Why should I? Give me one good reason."

Make it a good one Vey.

"Well, I have here this map, you see, and a flashlight. And I'm following something I never really have before."

There was no response at first, and I looked to my phone, thinking she might have hung up.

"Friday," she said. "Halloween. There's a costume party at my work. Some of my friends and patients will be there too, and if you want to show me something, you will be there. No excuses."

"Okay, I will, just please stop being so upset with me. I truly did not do anything to intentionally upset you or ruin things. I don't know what the future holds any more than you do, but I know I enjoy being with you and how you make me feel. For now, that's enough for me."

"Well I need a little more than that now, Vey. Show me you're not ashamed to be with me, show me something real, and honest, and maybe I'll forgive you."

For what? I wanted to demand this, but the haziness of my new reality led me to believe there were moments I had lost along the way, lost in the shadows and the enormity of their clever darkness. I only remembered blacking out once, that fateful first day in the park, but admitted it was possible similar lapses had transpired. Doubtful, but possible.

"Okay, fair enough. Thank you."

"But so help me, Veymont Addison, if you make a fool of me again, then I can't help you, and I don't know who can." Such harsh words from such a tender woman, and I was strangely excited by her firmness. I did not pass her off as someone to be walked on or pushed over, but I hadn't seen that side of her and wondered what else she was hiding.

"Umm, okay." I had no intention of hurting her or doing her wrong, least of all embarrass or make a fool of her, but apparently I accidentally had. I hoped I wouldn't again, but told myself if I did it once, it was possible again.

"Oh, and Vey..."

"Yes?"

"Wear a costume, or you're not getting in."

We both hung up and I sat in silence, looking around my kitchen, shaking my head. I had mere days to come up with a decent costume and show her I had no reservations of admitting to her, and all those with budding interest, of my honest adoration for the woman who helped me to see straight for the first time.

12

Do not think my vision problems ceased in these passing days, if I have failed to make more mention of them, for they did not, they only became more bearable. Since Claire's pep talk, their presence was not a cause for despair, but as I have said, a welcomed challenge, a formidable opponent. I managed to eliminate the unpleasant symptoms associated with them thanks to prescription refills and a consistent dose every twelve hours.

The large works I had begun developed unlike any picture I had seen before. Never having worked without the assistance of brushes, how could they have? I was amused to find myself unable to paint successfully *without* the distortions, and the days were split with sinuous periods of abstract reality and the normalcy I had walked blindfolded through for the previous forty-two years. Make that forty one; I crawled through the first.

I was a pirate come Thursday, after sampling on party store leftovers from the weeks leading up to the sugar infested holiday. The packages from which I was forced to choose had been rummaged, ransacked, and re-packaged to the best of the patrons' hurried and unconcerned abilities, half of the costumes missing their accessories. I had tried on several themes, none befitting me or flattering in the least. Upon trying on an afro wig for my amusement I was reprimanded by a store clerk who advised me the wigs were not to be tried on by anyone, and technically she could ask me to purchase the one I did, if she so chose.

"I'm sorry, I had no idea. I didn't—"

"That's what they all say!" She said, lacking the decency to look me in the eye during our entire exchange, instead pretending to be busy cleaning up after disrespectful patrons like myself.

"Uh, okay…" I shook my head. "How could I know that, there are no signs, and I haven't been in here before."

The plump woman, dressed as a witch, making her look more like a gothic Laundromat attendant, pushed aside a pile of wigs, displaced from their hooks and strewn about, revealing a laminated sign prohibiting the sampling of *any* headwear. "For sanitary reasons," she said, avoiding the sight of my reaction. "You understand." I did, but not her belligerence.

"My bad, I'm sorry. At least I didn't try to pee on it."

She sneered while a soft whinny escaped her mouth, and I pictured her to have the head of a horse, a more appropriate topside for a creature making such sounds.

The costume I settled upon to came furnished with a

black and red vest, matching pants, and an obnoxiously large pirate hat. I was lucky to make off with the hat, for I found many of the costumes were not equipped with the items depicted on their packaging. I still needed more—boot covers, a sword, a patch, any maybe even some facial hair to enhance the getup. I had no desire to try to grow anything appropriate, the five o' clock stubble that always covered my face would make no amendments.

Into an aisle filled with stiff, one-size-fits-all hats and assorted weapons, I continued my search, picking up an unrelated machine gun which caught my eye thanks to its realistic appearance. The price tag valued its worth at nearly sixty dollars, and I laughed at such egregious waste. Before I could place it back on the rack, the barrel turned to a warmed, black licorice and sunk down to the floor, the handle of the flaccid weapon still in my hands. Brief panic bubbled up through my neck, my ears grew hot with fear, and I found myself in a virtual shop of horrors. Claire's voice played back in my head and I closed my eyes to settle the anxiety, and I desperately craved licorice. I looked up to find an endless corridor of towering knives, guns, swords, and shields, stretching up to a hundred feet.

Laughing, I cried out "You have got to be kidding me!" I wished someone else could see what I saw, but I was all alone as usual. I put back the slop of gun the best I could and walked down the aisle whose end seemed nowhere in sight. I stopped in front of the police gear and picked up a pair of handcuffs now best suited for an elephant. Looking around, I spotted the enlarged pirate trinkets, quickly fetched the remaining pieces to my ensemble, and made my exit. The thirty-foot tall cashier looked at me funny, but then again he was wearing the mask of a Cyclops, so I excused him since he had little choice.

Outside the store, I smoked the vapors of my new life, the silence of the margins I danced in white as snow. The voices of the outside world I once heard with keen interest were now hidden in an underscore, cushioning the soundtrack that played through the grass and the wind and the thin layer of growth on my head. Serenity.

Bag of booty in hand, I took by foot, as became always, to the water, a bench undoubtedly in need of my seating and a river breeze in need of inhaling. The air was cool like an unused spoon and calmed my beating drum of a heart, while the cold, dusted ground below tried to rustle up what it could find, as if tuning up for a greater event.

These walks, I admit, must seem of questionable length, but having grown up in this city I can say you do not do without much inside its cozy arms, and the proximity its heart affords to most obligatory essentials leaves one without the need for efferent travels—for me at least, knowing the distance and duration from nearly any point in town to another, thanks to my having explored every inch of it on bicycle as a teen.

Friday I woke excited as if awaiting my first kiss, but later that day, staring into the mirror, it had turned out to be a costume party, and not a kiss at all. I drove that night for the first time in two months. My car, in dire need of a soapy shower, protested its awakening, and on the third try roared and purred the steady hum of a sleeping cat.

The roads were paved to their intended widths and lengths, much to my delight. Had they not, I would have taken a taxi, or asked Claire to help, but fortunately there were no setbacks. I expected at some point I would have to fight the illusions, but felt confident I would manage to adapt well enough so that no one would notice my handiwork within the corn field maze grown for my entertainment. I drove only because I had no desire to walk the streets dressed as a swashbuckling pirate, be it Halloween or not. I also had no desire to ride a cab in my flowing garb, my shattered ego still clinging for life to its supporting role in my decision making process.

The streets were bare, void of the green that had papered their walls for months, replaced with decaying crust, fallen to the ground in red, orange, and browns. It was half past seven and black and blue wounds filled the sky, the occasional streetlight dotting my route. A vampire and a princess held hands with their parents a few blocks away, and I noticed barely a handful of treaters before reaching the more residential reaches of the city. Where the brick apartment and office buildings ended, the comfort of a safe suburb where doors weren't locked set in quickly, and groups of goblins and gunmen littered the streets in a sucrose feeding frenzy. I felt a soft spot inside begin to warm while watching a mother pull her twins—no older than two—dressed as clouds in a red wagon. Their eyes brimmed with amazement and delight and I understood their surprise.

On the edge of town and outside of the Bright Horizon Center for Rehabilitation, I sat in my car, using the unlit visor mirror to check my face. Damn bulb. I had decided against faux facial hair or uncomfortable patches, opting only for a large set of hoop earrings I clipped on with ease. I came to party—like it was nineteen fifty nine—equipped with a dagger instead of a sword, and my brown boot covers met quite nicely with my roomy red pants. I took a deep breath, got out, and used the half-decent reflecting light from the parking lot poles to straighten myself in the side windows.

I had arrived. Unsure of what was to come, I knew at the very least my appearance would answer some questions for both Claire and myself. I had lived life too long in the safety of my calculations, and it was time to put the abacus away and let my heart lead me astray. She better be worth it, I told myself. She was, I argued back, stop talking such nonsense. I stepped forward, excited, to the beat of my fluttering heart and under the watchful eye of the silent owls hiding in the trees.

Ten feet from the covered walkway leading to the front door I wondered if I might find myself happy to be there twenty years in the future. I could already feel the awkwardness I knew to lie on the other side of the glass doors I targeted. When I finally came upon them and pulled one open, a single deep breath prefaced my entrance to the large foyer with tall, thick glass windows. I sighed and grumbled, took another deep breath and let it out. I flicked on a bright smile to cast assurances, and picked up a strut. I then decided I'd try to make the most of the situation, and regardless of her age, or anyone else's, Claire would still be there in all her majesty, drawing me in with her gentle magnetism.

The brassy vibrations from the recreation hall drew louder as I strolled closer. My nerves attempted to gain hold of me, but I resisted and fought them off with an attitude ripe with resolve and optimism. As insignificantly painful as the next three hours would likely be, I owed my efforts to someone I sincerely believed worthy of them.

A great bandstand melody greeted me upon entering the hall, and I looked for a basketball hoop. There wasn't one, and a fold up table to my left appeared to be my first stop. There sat an elder man and woman, dressed as Raggedy Ann and Andy, and I was surprised to find I remembered the characters names. They smiled the perfectly wide keyboard of parallel ivory which only dentures can project, and I marveled at how the manufacturers had yet to create a false gum that bore a true shade. A reel of raffle tickets lay, slightly unwound, before them. A scuffed, worn, gray lock box sat beside. "Take the money and run!" a voice buried in my head called out, and I recognized the devil's accent, paying it no further mind.

"Well hello young man…you must be Victor!" Ann said, rubbing her hands together as if she were being dangled over a fountain of youth in her bathing suit. Andy had frozen stiff the same smile he wore when I walked in, its height never faltering. I thought his face might be stuck.

"Veymont, actually." I put both hands down on the table and lightly drummed them on an invisible keyboard. "But you can call me Vey. Like hey!" I figured corny was appropriate.

"Well hello, Vey" said Ann.

"Hello" echoed Andy, still smiling. Yes, his cheeks apparently were stuck.

"I'm Nancy and this is my husband Emile."

I nodded. "It's a pleasure."

Someone cackled the loudest of laughs and we turned our collective heads in unison to see what was the fuss. It appeared from our view that Snow White had already sampled one too many Shirley Temples. She was on the floor pretending to be an animal of some sort, but not one I had ever seen before.

"Claire is over there," said Ann, "by the punch!" She turned on whisper mode and leaned her red mop head forward, using her lips to help spell out the words: "She's a naughty nurse, you know…"

"Of course she is. Nice to meet you both." I shuffled a ten dollar bill across the table, received a little blue ticket from Andy, and thanked them both. I headed out into the open room whose chairs had been pushed to the outskirts as if setting the scene for a junior high school dance. How fitting.

There wasn't a great deal of movement in the room, this I noticed right off. Most parties I attended held in common a purposeful energy marked by loud conversations, animated conjecture, and the possibility that something electric might erupt at any given moment. This wasn't most of those parties. The forty or so people in attendance mingled politely in hives of five or six, most seated and hushed, happily enjoying the throwback to their youths when nuclear weapons, fuel economy, and healthcare premiums were concerns of the spacemen who had traveled back unsuccessfully to stop a series of senseless assassinations from taking place. If only they could have worked out the bugs. I spotted Claire with a quick pan of the poorly lit room, which surprised me, considering a good portion of those in attendance couldn't see past their outstretched hands and could trip on half the things they wore.

She was smiling as usual, the menagerie in which she chatted eyeing me as she told them something flattering, I was sure, about me. I sauntered over and thought I recognized one of the two twenty something she-devils, or whatever they were, inappropriately dressed for the occasion. If any of the gentlemen present were to fall ill from heart complications or breathing malfunction, there was little doubt as to the likely catalyst. Claire's nurse outfit was no better, the white thigh-high fishnets she wore begging for someone to excuse her display and allow her to change into something more befitting her age.

Her doll figure filled the costume quite nicely; the white heels she wore gave her an added inch or two and her hair was pulled up and tied with a red ribbon, revealing her slender neck and my immediate thoughts were to take her into the massage room and make proper use of one of the tables.

"Excuse me, miss, I think I'm coming down with something. Do you mind taking a look?" I immediately wished I had been more original, but we were still rolling with corny, and luckily it had the desired effect. The group laughed politely, inspecting me carefully with high hopes in their expressions. "That depends," Claire answered, "is that a sword in your pocket, or are you just happy to see me?"

"No, it's a dagger, sorry. Don't make me have to use it."

"So you made it." she said, seeming relieved. She gave me a warm hug and turned me, as if directing a blind man trying to cross the street.

"This is Vey, everyone!" I was officially on display. "Vey, these are my girlfriends, Sherry and Chrissy." I made a concerted effort to maintain eye contact and avoid peeking at their uplifting chests, courtesy of their costumes. Did she say girlfriends or grandchildren?

"Hello," I said and shook both their hands, noting their

facial makeup had a tinge of glitter mixed in. Seeing these two beauties dressed to kill side by side with Claire reminded me I could be dating in a much younger tax bracket, but I did not care, although their presence was a bit distracting. I wondered if they were having as much fun as I anticipated I would. We were far from any singles nightclub where these girls could surely get lucky if they so desired, and it appeared half of their clothes had been stolen, or eaten by moths.

"This is Gertie," Claire said, and I followed her pointing.

"Hello."

"Helen,"

"Hiii."

"And Peter,"

"Howdy."

"And lets not forget Mary."

"Hi handsome," Mary said with a rather inviting tone.

"He's mine, Mary. Hands off!"

The group got a gas out of Mary, dressed as a nun, although the looks she gave me would surely have earned her several ruler whacks across the knuckles if any of her sisters had seen them.

"Can I offer you some punch?" Claire asked, her grin taking on a sinister form when she whispered "Its got a little something extra in it." Dean Martin sang out from a pair of speakers, and I though I would need something with a little more kick to get me through the night.

"Is there anything here with a little more kick?" See.

"I know Maggie brought wine and someone, uh, Dick I believe, brought vodka and cranberry...let me see where they are. You'll be okay by yourself?"

"I'm sure I'll manage..." To run off with one of your girlfriends. I feigned an inconvenienced sigh and said "Ugh, I suppose."

Claire flew away with invisible wings and I felt awkward, turning to the eye candy, expecting little in common of which to speak.

"So, how do you know Claire?" I asked

The one I believed to be Chrissy was proud to respond. "Oh, well, we all went to school together."

"Really now?"

"Yeah well, when we felt like going," Sherry added, giggling.

"Yeah, no kidding. You were the worst though Sherry!" she said, turning to her blonde-streaked sidekick. Sherry did not protest, just nodded and continued to sip something red through a straw.

"Wait, so what, like PT school or something?" I looked quickly over at Claire who commanded my internal focus, a brilliant light that did not exist paving her every step.

"No," one of the two said as if I had argued what day it was, "high school!"

The room wasted no time in helping to further my confusion and immediately began to rotate as if we were on a carousel, the horses replaced with statues of elderly people whose clothes had been stolen and replaced with joke shop leftovers. The short-sleeved shirt I wore underneath my vest became soaked under the arms within seconds of her response.

"High School?" I turned and asked with a shaky voice, trying to focus on the young women, but clearly unable to do so, looking back over at Claire with confusion. "How long ago was that?"

Claire drew nearer and as she did so I noticed her outline had changed, her arms had firmed, toned, and her chest had risen and grown, the white jacket she wore tighter and sexier than it had originally been and I instantly wanted to taste her legs.

She was only feet away now, a bottle in each hand which she held up one by one to show me my options, only she wasn't Claire. Her face looked the way I had tried to envision it so many times before, younger, tighter, softer. She looked like a child compared to the face I had known, or thought I knew. My heart took off and I could not catch it.

"Umm, eight, no wait, nine years ago," said Chrissy, while I stood on weak legs, and as the words left her mouth the room went from dim to red to black, and for the second time in as many months I collapsed at the feet of the same woman I still did not know.

13

I wish that I could tell you that it was all a cruel joke, that I was a pawn in a game resembling the ones played on the tables in the park, yet with much higher stakes and greater consequence. I wish I could tell you this, but the truth prohibits such fantasy from being put forth.

What say you? That I hold the proverbial pen and the power to stab forward whatever explanation I see fit, that I bear the sword, or dagger, and can put forth to paper the corresponding means to an end without the proper whereabouts or proof to back such claims?

Well I suppose somewhere in your peculiar reasoning you do pronounce a valid point, and if I saw fit I could lead you down a path which excites this tale and turns it into one of espionage, deceit, and trickery, but now that I have already revealed the inaccuracy of such untruths, it would be reckless of me to even begin to do so. Edit, you say? I could, but now that the words have been written I would find difficulty sleeping at night knowing my tale was not laid out accurately and truthfully, a consequence I cannot bear to endure, seeing as I need sleep desperately to function.

But wait! I think I might have found an option that will satisfy all involved and break storytelling tradition. I will make this short and sweet and try to stay within the lines I have drawn thus far. So, to appease those who yearn for an alternate ending filled with these angles, regardless of any lack of consistency with reality, I shall indulge in the notion, and deliver a brief synopsis of what did NOT happen once I came to at the Halloween party.

The following did NOT happen:

I awoke to find Claire hovering over me, a look of alarm and regret draped across her face. I sat up, confused.

"I didn't know they were going to tell you. They've been drinking. I'm sorry Vey. Here." In a scene reminiscent of one we had enacted before, she offered me a water. "You okay?"

"I think so, Claire, if that's who you really are. What the hell is going on?" I noticed her friends had relocated to the nearest corner of the room, and appeared to be concocting a scheme of great revenge, their eyes darting back and forth from each others sinister expression and over back at me.

"Can you see me?"

"I don't know who I see, Claire." I tongued my cheek. "The old lady mask is gone, if that's what you mean."

"I knew it would happen at some point."

"You had better start talking."

"We should have ended it from the beginning, but it wasn't my call."

On the verge of tears she rubbed my leg and looked into my eyes with dire sincerity. "I'm sorry Vey. I have some explaining to do."

Once on my feet, she escorted me outside where privacy could be found. My hat had fallen off and was left behind somewhere, but I could not care less. I looked foolish and I had apparently been playing the role for a while. We sat on one of the wooden benches that lined the entrance walkway. Taking a deep breath, she began:

"My real name is Victoria and I work for a drug company that does experimental testing for central intelligence."

I winced. "Victoria? Yeah that sounds real—wait did you just say the Government?"

"Not that they would admit any involvement, but..." She nodded.

"Go on." I urged, anxious and sincerely afraid of the words leaving her mouth.

"We were testing a new mix, through your water supply, one that would allow us to—"

"I knew it!"

"—to manipulate your vision from a mainframe, through a transmitter, and in turn, control you."

"Transmitter? What?"

"Yeah, you might have felt a pain in the back of your

neck when this began…" I felt a lot of pain, who could keep track? I reached for my neck and felt a burning rise from the depths of hell. "I injected a transmitter, now safely attached to your spinal cord."

"What!" I wondered if it was even possible. The world began to spin again.

"I know, I know, just relax, it's all okay—"

"Okay? Okay! This is far from okay!" I sat in silence. "What was the point of all this? What are you trying to do to me? Why me!"

"It wasn't about you. I don't know how you were selected, but I'm sorry. You have no idea. It's much bigger than you think." She stood up and paced in front of me. "Remember the girl in the liquor store?"

"Yeah, Hannah?"

"One of ours. Luckily you didn't question never seeing her in there before, seeing as it's a place you frequent."

"How did you—"

"Know you'd go there? We had four coverts, one there, one at the Saver Mart, one at the drugstore, and one at the adult, ahem, bookstore"

"Hey," I said looking at the ground embarrassed. "They have some out of print titles that are hard to find."

"Yeah, too bad there aren't any words in them."

I wanted to laugh with her, but the were more pressing emotions. I looked around, not seeing what my eyes saw, my mind's eye had taken over and I pictured each setting she had referenced. I remained dumfounded and dejected.

"So?"

"So there were no murders, we set those up—"

"What!" My eyes brimmed with rage.

"—and when we had you at the police station, try to tell me you wouldn't have danced the Macarena to get out of it."

"Yeah, I'm sure I would have done the Electric Slide if you asked me to, but aren't there easier ways to blackmail someone?"

"It wasn't blackmail." She sighed, the complexity of the situation straining her thoughts. "Its complicated. In controlled testing we had successes, but ugh, I don't have all the information. I'm just a small bit player in a big show."

"I don't know Claire—or Victoria—whomever you are," I stood up and got in her face. It was flawless but I shot down the thought with a sniper's accuracy: "What right do you have to play God and use people as pawns like that? You were literally destroying a life! And I'm sure I'm not the first! Come to think of it, the truck driver, that wouldn't have happened if you " I broke off and my head spun like a warped top. "I would rather have thought I was losing my mind than find that such...such cruelty exists!"

"I know, it seems pretty bad."

"Seems! Seems? No Claire, it's—Victoria, whatever! It's beyond bad! Let me ask you, was our little romance just an experiment?"

"No, no," she said, and I wanted to believe her. "When I

had lunch with you, I was supposed to try to get as much info as I could about you, but I quit your case the next day. We're not allowed to get personal, but I couldn't help it, you drive me crazy. I told them that! I have since the second I saw your picture."

"My picture?"

"You know, subject profile, bio, etcetera. Comes with photos." I nodded and widened my eyes. I was seeing very clearly. "Vey," She slid over and tried to put her hand on me.

"Don't—" I snapped, and stepped away, shaking my head. I looked up and searched the heavens for an answer that would not come. Looking down, out into the quiet parking lot frozen with shadows and lamppost half-moons shining on all the cars, I found it difficult to locate mine, the tears in my eyes blurring everything. It did not help matters when a large black hole suddenly opened up in the ground where the cars once were.

"Are we done here?" I asked, facing the cars.

"Only if you want to be." Her voice begged for forgiveness.

"And what about the drugs? Are we done with those?"

"I'll make a phone call. Just don't drink the water for a day or two. Or cook any pasta or anything with it."

I laughed, turning to the sad woman who looked like a stripper that had just been fired for meager dancing.

"Bye, Claire." She looked old again, the lines had returned to her face and her figure relaxed and she was still heavenly. I was glad. That was how I wanted to remember her.

I spun around and moved forward, and for the first time I wished the illusions had been real, so I could disappear into the black hole before me. I closed my eyes and stepped in.

The End.

Do authors actually end their stories with that tag line any longer? Did they ever? I cannot recall finishing a tale to find those silly words awaiting.

Again, I must reiterate that the events I have just made mention of did in no way truly take place, and their descriptions were nothing more than an attempt to appease those filled with the cravings of abstract reality, a whim I am happy to have satisfied seeing as I am a fan of the abstract. Now, back to seeing things with more clarity.

14

Back inside and before the false alternate ending, the lights came back on and I was moist all over with sweat. The room, littered with hushed voices, remained dark an unlit cave with cold, moist walls for a few seconds, then grew warm and bright—a nonexistent fool playing with the dimmer switch—and then to a comfortable glow. The sweat which I knew had been hot at first now cooled and refreshed my entire head and neck. My eyes were open, several degrees beyond normal, and more than ever.

"So I see." I grinned and took Claire's hand; she was knelt beside me in similar fashion after a fall I had taken not too long before. I kissed it with care and held it like a glass slipper as I pushed myself onto my feet.

"My goodness, are you alright honey?" It was the second time she had referred to me as such. I kept tally there.

"Never ever better, sweetheart." I hadn't been.

The room had picked up its volume, yet the music was still diffused and one could feel the apprehension lurking in the air. It seemed I was fine though; I felt refreshed and secure. Even I was surprised. I felt badly for the interruption, and understood in such a community that when someone went down, there arose suspicion they might not get back up. I held my hand up and called out to the multi-colored group, most of them relieved I was still ticking, and now whispering their theories for my demise.

"Sorry everyone!" I called out. "I haven't eaten all day, I'll be alright. Get back to dancing and ghost stories!" A smattering of polite laughter spilled out and before long it was business as usual, the cheap disco ball glistening, my eyes stuck on Claire.

She protested at first, citing my collapse as reason enough, but eventually gave in to dancing after I whispered in her ear that I wanted to hold her close to me. I couldn't tell you half the songs that played, with the exception of the occasional Sinatra, which we set our bodies in rhythm to.

"What is that look in your eye, Mr. Addison?"

"How old are you Claire?"

"Oh, so *now* he wants to know."

"Well maybe *now* it matters," I said with the most devilish of faces.

"And why is that?"

I twirled her, noting the burn at the base of her back was in fact a flowery tattoo, then coiled her back into my arms.

"Let's just say that I'm seeing things for what they really are. It's a new concept for me."

She paused, looked at me curiously, her eyes slits of white light, and said "Twenty eight." My head began to thaw.

"That's about what I thought. Just wanted to make it official."

Smiling, she noted it wasn't rocket science and that any forty-two year old could have figured it out.

"Forty-two huh? Lucky guess," I said.

"I might have been on your website bio page once or twice."

"Aha."

"Aha is a palindrome, you know?"

"You don't say?"

"So why didn't you stop and talk to me in the park last week? We waved and called you over, you looked right at me and laughed. Did you think that was funny? Do you know how much that hurt?"

I had a decision to make, one between truth and lies, and found I had no desire to fight alongside distorted truths any more.

"I was having one of my attacks, it didn't look like you at all. I had no idea who you were."

"Seriously?" she asked, surprised and struck with relief... "What did I look like, was I all twisted and deformed?" She made a funny face and it turned me on.

"Ha ha. No, you were beautiful, just a different version. I apologize, Claire. I was so confused when you wouldn't answer my calls. I was hurt too. I missed you."

She wrapped her arms in a closed circle around my neck and pressed her warmth into my waist. “I’m glad you can see me now.”

“I am too. And just so you know, I would never lie to you Claire, not after the first time. I’ll never make that mistake again.”

“I didn’t know there *was* a first time.”

Her cheeks were carved out of velvet sheets and her eyes swam in a puddles of green with twinkles of white light splashing about. Her skin held shades of auburn and saffron while the shadows that bounced on and off her hid her elegance and made want of its release in the pit of my stomach. As I studied her face I believed what I was saying. I would never lie to her again.

“The day we met, I told you my mania was caused by some unpleasant *noise* in my ears.”

“Ahh, yes,” she said nodding and looking up into her head for the scene.

“So I had, in fact, lied about that, so really our whole relationship began on a lie!”

“Well, you get one freebie.”

The music tempo picked up and I took the cue, squeezed her toned sides and lifted her up, high over me, then slowly slid her back down, closer, into me, until our lips met ever so gently with a wave of harmless needles.

As I enjoyed the ephemeral bliss that engulfed me my thoughts did what they did best and began to view the scene from every imaginable angle to find fault in the varying profiles. I still could not believe the reality of the situation and hoped it was truly reality. Was there necessity in seeking further proof of this most undeserving award? She had revealed her true age and I could clearly see she was a woman in her late twenties—what more did I need? I thought back to several of the things she had said prior to this evening, about children and marriage and career—all that had confused me to slight degrees—and with the force of a dragon's sneeze it all at once made sense, coming from this unfettered creature, this inimitable beacon of life.

I had fallen for her before the curtain came up, revealing her true identity. I had seen who she truly was, and wanted to be, and all she stood for. I drank from her cup of optimism and charity and I wanted more. Call it a drinking problem if you like, I don't mind. I had accomplished something never before imagined, I looked past the imperfections, the weathered signs of progression, of age, past my fears and insecurities and embraced the power that a heart built for resolve can emit. Without a manual or teaching, I learned how to blindly give to a being owed no devotion from blood or contract. I embraced the storm that scattered me, welcomed the change in the air and crept into the soft slippers awaiting my steps.

"Thank you for being honest," Claire said softly, somewhat apologetic. "I won't lie to you either…and on that note, there is something I must tell you."

I leaned back to look at her splendid face, her little nose nearly the same one I had been accustomed to, but with renewed freckles even cuter than before. The lines which stretched from the outskirts of her eyes had fallen away and with them the slight haze that had clouded her crystal eyes. I looked into them and tilted my head, a dog confused by its master's words.

"I don't know how to say this...it wasn't as if I planned it." She looked down and to her left, as if ashamed, embarrassed. I felt crushed without even knowing the reason why.

Her gaze moved up to my worried expression and told me after a long pause: "Vey, I'm preheating for a little loaf." She took a half step back and rubbed her stomach as if she were hungry, but I knew clearly what she meant.

She had to be kidding. I waited for someone to jump out of a cake to seal the deal.

"Are you sure?" I asked, knowing the question to be a knee jerk and pointless. "No, no, I'm, I'm sure you are! I...I meant, wow! Oh my!" I smiled, unsure what her feelings were, although I knew mine lie orbiting somewhere between cloud nine and asteroid forty-seven. I hadn't considered this happening, having ruled out the likelihood, thinking she were well past her fertile years.

"I know, it's crazy, I should have been more careful." She thought I was feigning my joy.

"No, no, don't put it on yourself." I brought her hands

together in mine, clasping them tight. "We were in it together. I wasn't using my head."

"Neither was I. I swear I don't normally do that, and I'm sure all the girls say that, but ask Chrissy and Sherry, they know. "

"Oh, don't be silly—"

"I wanted to tell you that there's something about you and I when we are together that...that just makes me so uninhibited. But I thought you might just take that as a line. I'm a fool."

"Well I'm just as foolish as you are, there's no double standards here." I noticed we had stopped dancing, and were the only two on the linoleum floor who had gone rogue. I picked up our steps and brought her in tight.

"Are you upset?" she asked my chest.

"No, not at all," I told her hair. "Strangely I'm excited and afraid and aroused all at once. Have you thought about what you'd like to do? I don't know how to delicately ask such a question seeing as I've never had to ask it before, but I assumed you had given it some thought."

"Well I always said I'd wait to get married before having kids, but now that it's in my lap, it feels a little different. I don't know what the right thing to do is. You drive me nuts and I can already envision some pretty magical days with you one way or the other!"

I was listening to her words, yet all the while I though to myself that if not for my condition I certainly would have been more careful, and this would never have happened.

I felt as though I should place the blame there, and was ready to voice my role, and admit who I thought she had been, but was quickly overridden with the fact that there was no blame to place, and that this was a gift, as many things of recent had actually been.

I knew my age was steadily climbing, and thus the chances of becoming a father were less and less with each passing day. Granted, there was still time beyond that day, perhaps a great deal, but I still enjoyed nimble reflexes and lacked the aches in my knees and back known to burden the elders of our species. That was enormous. I did not want to be a father who could not play with his children, so even if I could father a child into my fifties, would I want to? A gift, I thought, this is a gift.

All I knew was that it felt right, and it looked right. I tried to fight it, but found no sound reasons to resist. I also knew that the woman I held in my arms had another sixty to seventy years left to live, and not the twenty plus I had hoped she would have.

"Hey, why did you tell me to embrace it?" I asked, out of nowhere.

"What?"

"When I was having trouble painting, what made you say that?"

"Oh,...well, that's what I do. I welcome the challenges, the hurdles trying to slow me down, and I show them that they can't win regardless of their futile attempts. It's an everyday thing, Vey. The ups, the downs. Bring it on, I'm ready."

I was sure she was, too.

"And how did you learn this?"

"A wise old cat told me once."

"Oh yeah?"

"Uh-huh."

I held her tight and scanned the room, taking keen note of the two glaring red exit signs teasing me with their absolute temptation. I had come so far in such a short time, yet the comfort and familiarity of a path I had hoofed for so long without fail whispered in my ear.

"...never let anyone in..."

A song by the Clash played a muffled verse in my head. Should I? It wouldn't be the first time I ran from wild currents who threatened to suck me in and swallow me whole.

15

"It's cold."

This was my response to the man in bright blue. He had just asked if I was enjoying the snow. What more could I say?

"Do you have flowers?" he asked.

I, by any standard, had flowers, although I was not the guardian of their soil, spread thick around the edges of my corner-street town house. I had an interesting girl who took care of that.

"I do."

"Then does this not help water your precious flowers?"

Was this man kidding me? How did I meet these people? It was the middle of winter, what flowers was he talking about? Still, I could play nice. "I suppose it does, my friend and I am thankful when the sky cries white, as my flowers bring me such sweet smells and smiles."

This brightened the frail, hunched man, who appeared to be made from peanut brittle, and his eyes lit up to match his smile while he held an apparent winning lottery ticket tightly in his hands; I was sure he would buy another one with the reward, or perhaps even two if he struck a drop of pay dirt.

He turned when the cashier called him up and I looked over a foot downward, to the top of his head, the thin white dust ball posing as hair tangled in a foolish mess. I would always buzz my head—I had decided long ago—so as not to worry about encouraging such travesties.

The feeble elder looked to his left and right before sliding the ticket forward, not letting go until the clerk's hand took hold.

"Sorry my friend, I cannot cash that here." The uninspired cashier smiled apologetically and looked up at me to see what I needed.

I rolled my eyes, thinking he had been handed a bus ticket or a frozen dinner coupon. The old man, whose blue boots matched his long puffy coat with white trim, hung his head dejectedly and walked out, opening the door with his shoulder as the cold air smacked his already weathered face. He held the door open with his foot and turned back to me as I was placing a bottled water on the counter.

"Happy New Year" he wished me, in the saddest of tones.

"And to you too!" I said, heavy hearted from the disappointment which filled the doorway. The door closed and I looked out to see the sad, little man drop the ticket into the dirty, damaged barrel and clutch his arms tight to his chest before heading off into the unknown night.

"One thirty-nine."

I pulled a small fold of bills from my pocket and fetched a couple of singles.

"That man just won ten-thousand dollars." the middle aged clerk said, whose dark complexion or accent I could not originate. He said it so matter-of-fact that I almost let it go into the air which smelled of hot dogs and beef jerky.

"What?" My head jerked and I looked out again, knowing fully certain that his discarded fortune lie in a pile of hazardous waste, steps away.

"I can't cash that here, he's gotta go to the Lottery Commission." Philippine. I think that's what he was. Or Albanian. I had no idea, I was no good at that game. Regardless, he looked as though he might just fall asleep before I got my change back.

"Don't you get a cut of that if he wins?"

"I don't know." He didn't seem to care either.

I completed my transaction with the rush of a storm tide and hurriedly jumped out into the winter world. I opened my bottle, pausing and sipping quickly for effect, forgetting my thirst completely. With an inconspicuous eye I saw the clerk had moved onto his inventory count and could not see me reach down into the collection of filth to pluck the alleged treasure from its untimely death.

I ran a block each in opposite directions before spotting its rightful owner. It was nearly two in the morning and the streets were disheveled with party favors and uncoordinated mini-celebrations that popped up every so often. He wasn't hard to find and I stopped before confronting him, to inspect the ticket, and it was clearly a winner; the clerk had been right, and this poor man had believed his eyes to have failed him. I could relate.

"Excuse me!" I called out, half hoping he forgot the entire transaction, then remembered who I was now. He turned and produced a smile that told he was glad to see me, even without knowing my purpose. I produced the ticket and informed him of the mistake, and where he should go to claim his winnings. I went another step further and offered to take him the next morning.

"You sir," he said, tears glossing his gray eyes, and I wasn't sure if it was the cold or my news that brought them on, "are a gentleman of rare breed. The world needs more folks like yourself." If you had only met me two months ago, I thought.

"Do you have any kids?" he asked, checking my hand for a ring.

"No, I don't. Not yet, at least."

"Are you married?"

"Nope, managed to dodge that bullet too." I heard myself speak and I sounded like a me from a former life. Do work on that, I told myself.

"Well I hope you find your way to both someday, you will make an excellent role model." I thought that was the nicest thing anyone had ever said to me. "How can I repay you? I know! I shall split the winnings with you! It's only right." His wrinkled face was a muddled conglomeration of potholes and speckled fuzz. His innocent, aged smile was repayment enough.

"No, thank you though, that's all yours. You earned it."

"Well then, how shall I repay you?"

I looked down at this man and thought I might combust from the warmth our exchange had brought me. I loved the man I had become, or was now inspired to become, and could not wait for the rest of my life to unfold, the unplayed cards of each day abound with endless combinations.

"You already have, my friend. You already have."

Several blocks away I proudly stood on the steps of the locked art museum where my newfound gifts were on display. I had managed to secure a more appropriate viewing site after some people in-the-know caught wind of my new talents. Happy New Year, I wished myself without a spoken word, unable to erase the smile stamped on my face. The night was over and my life was just beginning. "Veymont the Finger Painter" had brought a new voice to abstraction. It wasn't "Veymont the Great" but I'd take it. The critics would soon raise me to the rafters, where I would hang overlooking a world of prisms. Success had never tasted so sweet, especially with an impending delight to enrich with it.

16

July came in true New England fashion: packing heat. I lie on the couch flipping through a cheap, yet trendy, home furnishing catalog, the air conditioner humming quietly to itself across the living room, when Claire, in the adjacent den and perched in front of the computer, called me out. “Honey, come look at this!”

“What?” I hollered back, moving only my eyebrows and lips, intently fixed on a desk with hidden drawers. I thought she was looking at some new breed of flowers she wanted to plant. She was always busy playing in her flowerbeds.

“I can’t help you see things with sounds when I ask you to *look* at something, silly boy.”

“What? I have no idea what you just said. Was that even a sentence?”

“Honey!”

There is a quirky, loving, unspoken dance that always seems to be shared with the two of us whenever we are together, with or without our feet moving.

“Vey!”

"You don't have to yell," I said, already in the den and over the bare shoulder of the third version of Claire I had been fortunate enough to see.

"Oh! Well hello..." she said, turning with a moan to look up at my chin. She cocked her head to the right, allowing me to read. I looked at her belly first. It looked as if she had stuffed a red kickball under her shirt. I then scanned the words quickly, then with more care when I took serious note of her find. After thirty seconds of me mouthing the words and Claire waiting for me to kiss her, she chimed in and said "Alice In Wonderland Syndrome. Who would have thought?"

"Alice Cooper," I whispered.

"Huh?"

"Is it even real?" I asked, still reading on about the condition whose existence my doctors had failed to pick up on and was now injecting me with newfound optimism.

"It seems legit. Hey, didn't you say you saw a little white rabbit in the cemetery a while back?" I had forgotten about my little friend, and now remembered I liked him.

"I did, yes."

"Just like Alice In Wonderland."

The projector spooled back and I thought about the book, one I had read several times long ago, and like rising bread I saw that it was similar, and that several other excerpts from the tale bore eerie resemblances to parts of my recent adventures.

"Wow..."

She got up using the desk to sturdy herself and I held her arm, although it did nothing of its intended purpose to help her in any way. I tried.

"I love you," I said to the woman I would squeeze blood from rock for.

"Love you too, LuVey."

We exchanged places, and she shook me off when I tried to help her into the other room. I know when I'm being of no use. Luckily so does she.

"Shoosh. Go read, I'm fine. An intense game of solitaire upon my belly awaits." She kissed me right on the kisser. I pictured the card game she had initiated once as a joke, claiming that her stomach made a sufficient card table when reclined to a specific degree.

"Thank you." Cue kiss on forehead. "You are a goddess."

Time stood still while I sat and read every line of a dozen different websites which carried any mention of the secret disease whose validity I still had yet to establish. I could not believe what she had found! The distortions, the headaches, the depth deformities, it was all there. Some of the things people saw appeared differently, their shape and size on different scales, but all in all it was there.

It seemed as though the cure did indeed lie in the headaches and my doctor had been right all along. "Sweetie, this is nuts, these people have all experienced the same things. Some even worse!" I clicked repeatedly, scrolling, reading excerpts from a blog dedicated to the discussion of the obscure impairment, a form of migraine aura. "And it seems as though that if I keep switching my candy that eventually one of them will make it all go away. Well that's what it says, who knows." Claire failed to respond, and I tried to engage her. "But we don't want that now do we? What's the fun in that?" I had already tried eight, and thought that was plenty. It was okay, I didn't have any pain anymore. So what if I had to watch life through a glass of water sometimes. I got up and came to find her asleep on the couch, most likely dreaming of unicorns and sunshine pies.

"Oh, Claire, you silly, silly girl." Her stomach was covered with cards, a scattered mess of a game in progress. It did not resemble solitaire, but fifty two pickup, a gag of a game that can usually only be pulled once on the wise.

I watched her rise and fall with each cushioned breath, her mouth open a hair, and I found it most arousing. She was utterly silent and after several timeless, comforting minutes I gasped, as a pool of clear liquid settled in under her and saturated the cushions. I began to panic, thinking her water had broken, but my fears were silenced when I noticed an uncorked bottle of water tucked between her legs. My eyes, who had a history of exaggeration, were playing their same old card tricks on me, and this one had gotten me good!

I plucked the bottle from its resting place and shook my head, laughing inside, still surprised at times by the oddity of my days. I left the cards, thinking there might be some intricate game at hand that I was oblivious to, but more importantly that it looked cute, so I returned to my desk, sat, and read on:

"At times I feel as if things are filled with helium, and they expand until I can't see anything else. The air gets sucked out of the rest of the world and into everything I look at."

I found myself nodding at the words as if they could read my affirmation.

"While I'm in the shower, it looks as though I am standing on a cliff, the rain falling for miles and miles, the suds from my body pouring over the ledge into oblivion."

My neck stiff and my eyes sore from staring, Claire mumbled something unintelligible from the next room. I glanced to the left as though her words might crawl up the desk and reveal their true meaning to me.

"Oh, no...Vey..." she said in a groggy voice.

"What's that, dear?" I replied casually.

"My water."

"Water" I said, still reading the screen, unable to snap out. I whispered it again, "Water," and thought about the word water. Wohter. Wahter. Whater. You could write it several ways I thought. Oh, her water!

"Water? Oh! Right here." I grabbed the bottle from the desk in front of me, making sure the cap was sound, and stood, pivoting to bring it to her in the next room. She was sitting up, holding her stomach, looking up at me with an apologetic stare. The cards were strewn on and about her, on the couch and floor, a giant pile of leaves she had fallen into, and I started to laugh, until I realized my eyes had not been playing their games.

"Oh, *that* water, my darling." I nodded and calmly helped her up, into her shoes, and out into the car for the biggest day of both of our lives. A storm cloud leveling a city to crumbled ruin is rumored to rear its head upon the man who forgets his lady's hospital deliverance bag. I, of course, remembered the sacred bag, and the skies were kind.

I moderated an internal discussion with myself in regards to safety procedures while driving to the hospital. If in the event of an Alice attack, I would lower my speed and do my best, unless I felt that as a passenger I would not have felt safe within the arena of my road handling skills.

Fortunately, the trip was uneventful, and I kept my calm, secure in the happiness that had wallpapered the insides of my days.

The hospital was about fifteen miles away, and Claire was stable, glowing in the lights that flickered off her cheeks through the windshield.

"You have been so, so calm, Vey. I am quite impressed!" She tilted her head and nodded, an approving smirk present.

I kept my sight focused ahead of me and patiently awaited the gold star to be put on my forehead. Hey, I earned it. "Oh, my heart is going to explode any minute, so you might want to get a towel or something, in case I get any on you."

Laughing, she put a hand on my outstretched arm. "I am honored to be doing this with you."

"And I you, baby."

"You know, *our* baby is going to be one lucky kid, but I hope he or she doesn't melt from all the love we pour on it."

"Heheh, well I'm sure *he* or *she* will be okay even if they do."

Minutes later we were calmly rushed down a corridor with a worn, faded stripe of red tape splitting the otherwise gleaming floor down the middle. It eventually took a right towards the emergency room while we hooked left to the maternity ward. We passed a vending machine and my mouth watered at the sight of chocolaty delights under lock and key.

Hospitals were never my favorite place, not that they are a favorite of very many, but its very opening scene begins with the long face of a check in nurse—an un-phased, torn reminder of the death and dismemberment crossing the threshold from day to day. I told myself that if I ever owned a hospital I would implement a "no frown zone" in its waiting rooms. I understand the unlikelihood of sound success being achieved in such a zone, but again I feel boundaries need to be pushed.

I was forced to get over my distaste for hospitals roughly five hours later when my heart began to sprint rows of hurdles.

I was afraid.

There are feelings we experience every day, sensations of happiness or sadness or indifference, and many others. Within these divisions like countless versions, different emotions that we are struck with from time to time, all of them familiar, having felt their roots before at some point. The feeling which took over me was none I had known to any degree and it grew to ice in the core of my soul and then melted from the power of a heart built for resolve. My tongue tingled, my throat tightened, and I nearly accomplished a fainting trifecta when not one, but *two,* heads emerged from Claire's outstretched legs.

"It's a girl!" The doctor declared. Not *girls*, just one. I should have guessed so.

The rollercoaster car in my stomach came to a screeching stop and Claire held our little swan of a girl in her arms, while her pale face ran wet with tears and sweat, her hair pushed back and into the mountain of pillows which propped her up.

"Say hi to your daddy." Claire's swelled smile mirrored my own as I allowed my eyes to absorb the most beautiful sight they had been privy to.

The doctor watched us proudly, another successful entry into the world at his skillful, veteran hands. "You and your wife have a beautiful little girl there."

"Oh she's not my—" I broke off and searched Claire's face, holding her stare and wishing she were. "—not *yet* my wife, but hopefully, if she'll have me, it won't be long."

She looked at me, her already beaming face even brighter, her eyes perfect slits of white light in and endless night sky, when warm tears began to stream single slides down her cheeks again. “So I see.” she whispered.

No, so *I* see.

CPSIA information can be obtained at www.ICGtesting.com
Printed in the USA
LVOW051157210912

299620LV00002B/212/P

9 781608 367566